The cab filled with Emma

Logan fought to open his eyes. He prayed—*God, please let Emma be okay*—but soon his prayers faded from his lips, and he sank back into the darkness.

He woke again and realized he was pressed against the steering wheel. Shards of glass covered his body. The airbag hung limp like a deflated balloon. Memories flooded his mind: the sudden impact and piercing screams, the jolt to his body as they hit the ditch, Emma's voice... *Emma?* He turned in his seat, hot pain searing through his neck muscles. Fear rose up from his chest as he fought to free himself from the seat belt.

Emma was gone!

Then footsteps outside. "Help me. I'm in here. Help—" He fumbled with the clasp, adrenaline pumping through his body. The belt was stuck. *Come on, open, open.* The footsteps stopped outside his window. Terror silenced him.

He rolled his gaze upward and saw not a friendly face but the cold black barrel of a gun...

Susan Furlong grew up in North Dakota, where she spent long winters at her local library scouring the shelves for mysteries to read. Now she lives in Illinois with her husband and children and writes mysteries of all types. She has over a dozen published novels and her work has earned a spot in the *New York Times* list of top crime fiction books of the year. When not writing, she volunteers at her church and spends time hiking and fishing.

Books by Susan Furlong

Love Inspired Suspense

Lethal Wilderness Trap
Murder in the Appalachians

Visit the Author Profile page at LoveInspired.com.

MURDER IN THE APPALACHIANS

SUSAN FURLONG

Susan Furlong
2/18/2025

LOVE INSPIRED SUSPENSE
INSPIRATIONAL ROMANCE

LOVE INSPIRED® SUSPENSE

INSPIRATIONAL ROMANCE

ISBN-13: 978-1-335-98053-3

Murder in the Appalachians

Copyright © 2025 by Susan Furlong

Love Inspired
22 Adelaide St. West, 41st Floor
Toronto, Ontario M5H 4E3, Canada
www.LoveInspired.com

Printed in Lithuania

Recycling programs
for this product may
not exist in your area.

MIX
Paper | Supporting
responsible forestry
FSC® C021394

And the Lord, he it is that doth go before thee;
he will be with thee, he will not fail thee,
neither forsake thee: fear not, neither be dismayed.
—*Deuteronomy* 31:8

To our son, Patrick:
I thought of you when I wrote this story.

ONE

Autumn's yellow-and-orange-tinged Appalachian Mountains painted a picturesque scene from the highway, but up close, under those trees and alone on the trail, the shadowy woods seemed menacing. Emma pulled her jacket tighter, wishing she was back in DC and her snug apartment, where she could hole up, shut out the rest of the world and wallow in her grief. But her twin brother's death was shrouded in questions, and she needed answers, so she continued to trudge along the trail, dodging roots and branches, until she reached the clearing.

Nothing about the old fishing cabin had changed—the same weathered siding, rusty metal roof and porch shady enough to provide a little reprieve on the hottest of West Virginia summer days. She eyed the wooden rocker tucked in the shadows, and childhood memories surfaced: tree forts and fireflies, lazing the evening away listening to Mama rocking back and forth, and her and Daniel as children tossing and whirling in the crinkly leaves of autumn. She shook her head and kept walking. Memories were a rabbit hole she couldn't afford to go down right now. She needed to stay focused and alert.

She kicked through the leaves to the side of the house and found the key where it always was, under the rock by the woodpile. Gripping it in her fingers, she climbed the steps onto the porch, then paused. The sighing of the wind in the treetops, a bird's sweet chirps, the cracks and pops of small rodents scurrying through fallen leaves—nothing but the sounds of nature, but still something seemed off. Goose bumps pricked her skin. She rubbed them down, told herself that it was nothing, that it was just her imagination, and unlocked the cabin door, pushing it open slowly.

Everything remained as Daniel had left it: a pair of mud-caked boots rested by the door, a fishing pole propped at an angle in the corner, an old shirt tossed over the back of a chair. She felt the fabric, soft and thin from years of use, and pressed it to her face, inhaling a hint of wood smoke and exhaling a jagged breath. Not even thirty, Daniel had had his whole life ahead of him before he was fatally shot. Officially, he'd been one more police officer killed in the line of duty. Unofficially, she suspected more to the story.

She shivered again, an uneasy feeling crawling over her as if she was being watched. Silly, she thought. She was alone, and there was a task to finish, so she shook off her fear and crouched next to the marred wood table. She removed her cell phone and replayed Daniel's last voicemail message to her: *Hey, sis. Tried calling a couple times, but... Anyway, I'm at the cabin, just stopped by before my shift, and...well...this may sound weird, but a while ago I stashed some valuable info about a cold case until I needed it. Now things are getting strange here, and I don't know who I can trust. I can't say too much on a message, so call me when you get this, okay? I'll explain everything.*

Guilt washed over her. She'd been caught up in a deadline from her editor and had her phone turned off. If only she'd answered, maybe he'd still be alive.

"I'll find the truth, I promise," she half whispered as

she removed her pack, took out a small pocketknife and leveraged the blade along the edge of the third floorboard from the wall. Their private childhood "treasure stash," as they called it. If there was any truth to her gut feeling that Daniel's death was more than a random shooting, it would be here.

The board popped loose, and inside was a waterproof bag, and inside that, a leather-bound notebook. She turned it over in her hands and leafed through the pages. *Daniel's police notebook.* She stood and carried it to the front window for better light, skimming one page, and another. He'd recorded several investigative notes, calls he'd responded to, a couple of incidents involving teens, a domestic call, a drunk driver. She scowled, glancing back at the hiding spot. Nothing unusual in his notes, so why was it hidden?

She turned to leave, and her gaze caught on a small black box mounted near the door. A security camera. Daniel hadn't mentioned getting security cameras. Did he have trouble with break-ins? The cabin was usually unoccupied, and there was nothing here of value to take, but the place wasn't visible from the road, so it'd be easy to… Her head jerked up as a flash of movement outside the window drew her attention. Something wove between the trees at the edge of the clearing. She squinted. A deer? Or a coyote? She'd seen them before. Mangy things. But then a form took shape, not animal, but human, and a man emerged from the tree line, dressed in camo with a gaiter covering his face. He carried a pistol.

Emma crouched and scurried back to her backpack, cramming the notebook inside and fumbling with its zipper. She peered back through the window. The man was moving closer, so she fell to all fours, crawling across the floor, splinters from the rough wood tearing at her jeans until she reached the back door. Her heart hammered in her throat. She could run for cover in the forest behind the cabin, but the span to the tree line seemed impossibly long. She'd be out in the open, exposed and a moving target, but footsteps sounded on the front porch, the doorknob jostled, and she had no choice. She was out of time.

She sprang up and bolted out the back door for the woods, her feet exploding against the ground, her focus on reaching the safety of the trees. Behind her, an angry male voice pierced the air. She didn't dare look back, but pumped her arms harder, willed her legs to go faster. A series of gunshots reverberated in her eardrums and bullets tore into the dirt next to her. Her instinct was to duck, cover her head, cry even, but she pushed forward until she burst into the woods, not slowing even though branches clawed her skin and tore her clothing.

Another shot splintered the bark of a tree in front of her. She startled and jerked to the right, sucking in her breath, before plunging down a steep ravine, her arms doing the breaststroke against the thick underbrush. Her lungs burned, and dark spots formed at the edge of her vision, while footsteps crashed behind her.

She kept going until the trees thinned and more light filtered through the forest canopy. Dread crept over her. She was exposed again. A sitting duck. A bullet could hit her at any second, but over the pounding of her heart she heard rushing water. The river. *Maybe if I can get to the river...* She broke through the trees and into the open, using everything she had to propel herself forward. She finally reached the river's edge and stopped, staring at the water as it swirled and bubbled over a rocky ledge to the fast-moving, murky abyss below. Dangerous, deadly maybe, but behind her, leaves scraped and twigs snapped. He was getting closer. She cast one last glance over her shoulder, before tightening the pack on her shoulders and slipping into the river.

Ice-cold water shocked her muscles and whisked her from the bank, the weight of her pack and the power of the current sucking her under. Muddy water filled her ears, her throat, and clouded her vision. She fought to breathe, breaking the surface and gulping mouthfuls of air as her body slammed into jagged boulders. The garbled sound of gunshots rang overhead, and bullets sliced the surface of the water inches from her face. She managed one more intake of air, relaxed her body and allowed the current to carry her downstream.

Logan Greer cast his line and watched his fly dance over the water, breathing in the mountain air and exhaling the stress he'd stored over the past few months. There was something truly poetic about fishing, the sun gleaming on ripples of water, the fish waiting in shadowed pools, and the way a perfectly cast fly kissed the water. He sighed. It'd been a difficult month, which was his own fault. He'd been pushing himself at the hospital, taking on extra shifts in the ER, all while attending fundraising events to keep up with the never-ending bills and supplies needed to run his free clinic. Plus, his caseload at the clinic on his supposedly "free" hours had increased with the community's opiate epidemic issues. Exhaustion had caught up to him a few weeks back at the worst time possible—while attending a patient in the ER. Fatigue had triggered a flashback of his military service as a combat medic in Afghanistan, sending him into a downward spiral of unwanted memories and causing him to make a mistake that would forever haunt him. He'd spent the last three weeks regretting that mistake, but now he forced himself to redirect his thoughts. He'd taken this break not to dwell on the past, but to rest and reconnect with God.

Even as a child, this mountain and this river had been his reprieve from the rest of the world. It was a magical place, especially in the fall when the tree-filled valleys exploded with vivid rusts and oranges. He drew in a deep breath of crisp, sharp air and glanced upward to where a hawk scrolled broad cursive strokes over the blue sky, and for the first time in weeks, peace settled over him. He'd made the right decision, he knew, coming out here to spend a few days in the woods.

He cast again, but this time a gust of wind blew through the gulch and carried his fly, snagging it on the far bank. He yanked, trying to free it. No luck. Reeling in the slack, he waded through knee-deep water, following his line to where it wound around a cluster of driftwood. He bent to untangle it, gently coaxing the barb of the hook, when a splotch of color on the river's bank drew his gaze. He shielded his eyes and squinted. *A woman?*

He clamored through the water, slipping on the moss-slicked boulders, tossed the pole onto the shore, and then grasped at the rocky bank to hoist himself up the slope. A woman's body was there, crumpled on the riverbank, arms wrapped around her legs, long hair plastered to her face, her eyes only half-open. There was no response when he called out to her. He felt the cold flesh of her neck for a pulse, and found one, slow and faint, but steady. Was it possibly hypothermia? Even in early September, night temperatures could drop into the fifties, maybe even the forties. People didn't realize that it was possible to freeze to death in forty-degree weather, especially after submersion in cold water. At least her clothing had dried in the sun, warming her skin a bit. Still, her core temp wouldn't have been impacted enough, and if he didn't act quickly, she wouldn't make it.

He scooped her into his arms and carried her back across the river. Her body hung limp with the long curve of her neck exposed as her head lolled from side to side against his shoulder. She was small and thin, the sharp angles of her bones protruding through her clothing. Reaching the other side, he hurried down a short path to his cabin and rested her gently on his couch. He pushed long red strands of hair from her face, noticing cuts on her cheekbones and along her jawline. Her full lips were slack and bloodless. Feeling for a pulse again, his hand brushed against her shoulder and came away bloody. Gently, he peeled back the collar of her shirt. A deep cut lined the edge of her shoulder.

He needed to avoid any infection, but right now the real threat was her declining core body temperature. He piled blankets by the hearth, rekindled the morning fire until it blazed. Gently, he removed her boots and socks and scooped up the warmed blankets and tucked them around her, exposing only her shoulder wound. He gathered basic medical supplies and cleansed her wound with antiseptic-soaked gauze before fitting a tight bandage. After stoking the fire, he piled more blankets on top of her, snugged up to her neck, until she was nothing more than a small face in a cocoon. Then he waited. And prayed. And wondered who she was and how she'd ended up on the bank of the river.

Emma fought through the thick fog in her mind and forced her eyelids open. She was in a cabin of some sort, on a couch, her body weighted down by blankets. She stayed still, turning her head slightly to scan the room, noting its simple kitchen with shelves stocked with dry goods, a crudely built table with two chairs, and a floor-to-ceiling stone fireplace. Like Daniel's cabin, but...this wasn't Daniel's place. Where was she? How did she get here?

Fuzzy details resurfaced: the notebook, gunshots, the river, her backpack... *Where's my backpack?* She struggled to push herself upright, falling back again when the cabin door popped open. She remained stock-still, eyes open only a slit. A strange man came in, with short dark hair and wearing jeans and a long flannel overshirt, a bundle of wood in his arms. He dumped it near the fireplace and threw a couple of logs on the fire. Flames reared up, the wood hissing and cracking, and he stood back, shrugging out of his flannel and warming his hands over the fire.

The man who chased her through the woods?

A weapon. That was what she needed. Anything to defend herself. Her gaze rolled about the room and settled on a heavy cast-iron pan hanging from a rack near the sink. She slid one leg out from under the blankets, eased her body to sitting, then to standing. If she could get to it before he—

"Hey, you're awake. How are you feeling?" He'd turned around and was staring at her.

She froze, then tried to take a step, determined to get to the pan, but her feet tangled in the discarded blankets and the room spun. She blinked and tried to keep focus. The man was walking toward her now and fear gripped her.

"You'd better stay put for a little while," he was saying. "I found you by the river. You were suffering from hypothermia."

She sat back down and looked at her bare feet. Her boots were gone. Anxiety pricked her skin at the thought of him touching her. "Where are my boots?"

He pointed to the fireplace, where her boots stood on the hearth with her socks carefully spread on the floor. He eyed her for a couple of beats, and then backed up and crossed to the cookstove and poured a mug of coffee. "Here, this will make you feel better."

The mug trembled as she brought it to her lips. She sipped, then gulped, allowing the hot liquid to burn its way to her stomach.

"Logan Greer," he said, seeming to relax a little. "Like I said, you were on the riverbank suffering from exposure. Thank God that I found you when I did."

He continued fumbling his words while she sipped the hot coffee. Her mind started to clear.

"It's really a miracle," he continued. "I just happened to be in the right place at the right moment. I usually don't come out this time of year, and...uh, you're probably hungry."

He rifled through a cupboard and came back with a protein bar. After she'd taken a couple of bites, he asked, "What's your name?"

"Emma." She felt better. The dizziness had subsided. "Where are we? Is it still Tuesday?"

"Yes." He smiled.

She liked his smile, and his dark, sincere eyes, but his gaze was intense and a little unsettling. She didn't trust him. Not a bit.

"We're about a mile and a half from the West Trail access," he said. "Not far from the Blackwater River. That's where I found you, at a shallow point. River Falls is the closest town. It's about fifteen miles or so from here."

"In the middle of nowhere, then." How far was she from Daniel's cabin? The Jeep?

"You have a nasty gash in your shoulder. I cleaned and dressed it, but you might need an antibiotic, maybe stitches. My truck is parked at the trailhead. If you're up to it, we should get you to the clinic in town. I'm a—"

"Where's my backpack? I need my backpack first."

"Backpack? You didn't have one when I found you."

She pushed up from the makeshift bed again, and another rush of dizziness hit her. He was suddenly there, his hand on her elbow, steadying her. "Hold on. Where are you going?"

She jerked her arm away. "I need to find my pack."

Whatever was in the notebook was important. It had to be. Why else stash it in their childhood hiding place? She was convinced that Daniel had died because of it.

"I'll help you. But first tell me what's going on. How did you end up in the river? Did you fall in or were you rafting or—"

"Please, I need to find my pack. It's important."

"Okay. I'll go back to the river and look around for your pack. You stay here and rest."

"No. I'll go." She pushed past him and headed for her boots and socks, struggling to slip the socks on and keep one eye on him. He'd moved to a set of coats hanging on pegs near the door, handing Emma her jacket. Her shoulder screamed with pain as she stuffed her arm into the sleeve, her fingers fumbling over the zipper, her hands stiff and clumsy. She remembered her phone in the pocket and pulled it out and tapped the screen. Nothing. It was dead, maybe ruined forever.

"There's no cell service up here anyway," he said.

Her head popped up. He was staring at her again.

"Are you in some sort of trouble?" he asked. "I might be able to help you."

She averted her gaze and spied a Bible splayed open on the hearth. He must've been reading it while she slept. That should be a comfort, but instead her stomach soured. She hadn't much use for God since He let Daniel die. Didn't have much use for this man right now, either. The sooner she got out of here, the better.

"Like I said, my truck is down at the trailhead. If you feel strong enough, we can—"

"That's okay. I'm good." She slipped into her boots. The damp lining sent a chill through her. She clenched her jaw against the shiver and turned toward the door.

"Please wait. You're in no shape to be out in the woods."

Stumbling down the porch steps, she headed straight for the tree line. Not that she had any idea where she was going, wasn't even sure where the river was, only that she had to find Daniel's notebook and that she could trust no one. She slowed a moment, knowing that making panic-filled decisions wouldn't help her. She took in a breath and listened, turning her head slowly. Yes, the river was just beyond those trees. She made her way to the water's edge, hoping the pack had washed ashore, but she scoured the bank, searching up- and downstream for over an hour with no luck. It could be anywhere by now.

Fatigue enveloped her body. Her breath became shallow and labored, her shoulder hot with pain. She'd left the man's cabin without bringing water or food, without thinking things through, and every sound she heard, every snap and pop, sent fear through her. "I am strong enough," she whispered and soldiered on, not giving in to her anxieties, until she finally spotted her pack snagged between two rocks in the river.

Her spirits lifted. She'd found it! She plunged in, reaching out with her good arm. "Got you!"

Daniel would be proud. She lifted her head in triumph, but her elation was instantly scattered by fear. A man stood on the opposite side of the river. Not Logan, but the thin form of the man who'd shot at her. Their gazes met for one terror-filled second, before she turned, scampered out of the shallows and ran. The wet pack weighed heavy and cumbersome in her hand. She swung it onto her back and forced her bad arm into the strap, crying out in pain, but not stopping. She couldn't stop. Once again, her life depended on outrunning the man.

Behind her, water splashed as the thin man crossed the river. She knew he'd easily overcome her as soon as he hit solid ground. She made it back to the woods, trying to retrace her steps to the cabin. Right? Straight? She hadn't marked a trail. *Stupid, stupid, stupid!* She shouldn't have left the cabin. She should have listened to Logan, but she had to—

An arm from behind yanked her off her feet, and a hand slid over her open lips, the taste of sweat and salt bitter on her tongue. She bit down, hard, and kicked and flailed her arms, bucking against his grip, but he was bigger and stronger, and the air pushed from her lungs as he pulled her tightly against his body.

TWO

"Quiet!" Logan hissed into her ear and prayed she would stop panicking. He pushed her to the ground and under a pile of fallen trees, partially covering her body with his. "He's coming. Don't move."

Emma's pulse pumped in rhythm with his own frantic heartbeat, while the earthy, decayed smell of rotting wood stung his nostrils and an insect scurried across his neck, under his collar, and pricked his skin. He gritted his teeth and willed himself to stay still as he heard the rustling of leaves nearby. Turning slightly, he rolled his eyes upward. The man stood a few yards away, gun in hand as he scanned the trees like a predator bent on the kill.

Fear-induced adrenaline flooded Logan's body. His instinct was to fight, run, do anything except lie helpless and vulnerable. But there was no way they'd outrun a man with a gun, so he remained locked in place, silent and still in the underbrush of the forest, while seconds ticked away, slow and seemingly never-ending. Who was this man? Why was he after Emma?

Finally, the man moved on. Logan waited, listened, until he could no longer detect any movement. Quietly, Emma started to get to her feet. "He's heading toward my cabin," he whispered. "We'll have to go a different way."

She readjusted her pack and didn't resist as he led her deeper into the forest, holding her hand and picking each silent step carefully. "Stay close," he told her. "I'll get you out of here." Her palm was sweaty, her face pale and her shirt soaked with sweat. Fear held her in its grip, and he didn't know if she could make it. "You can do this, Emma. It's not far."

"I don't even know where we are."

Her voice sounded small and fragile. "It's okay. Trust me. I know the way."

The trees thinned and the trail grew wider, and finally they broke through the woods and stumbled into the parking area. They scrambled into his truck, Logan breathing easier as the engine cranked over. He turned to Emma. "We made it."

A gunshot exploded through the back window.

Emma cried out. He hunkered low over the steering wheel, jammed the gear into Drive and floored it.

Peeling out of the trailhead lot, he raced down the road, putting distance between them and the shooter. "Are you okay?" he asked, his gaze darting from his rearview mirror to Emma. She'd buried herself in the passenger seat, glass shards covering her back. She was trembling. "Emma? Are you cut?" He reached over and brushed a piece of glass off her back.

She flinched and pulled away. "I'm okay."

He'd only known her a short while, but even he could tell she was lying. She still didn't trust him. "We're about twenty-five minutes from River Falls. I can get you medical attention there." He pulled out his phone and checked it. No service yet.

She reached for her pack and winced, her injured shoulder pressing up toward her cheek.

"Is the pain bad?" he asked.

"It's not good."

"That man back there, who is he? Why was he shooting at you?"

She unzipped her backpack with her good arm and pulled out a waterproof bag. Her shoulders relaxed as she removed a small notebook. It was dry. She flipped through the pages, engrossed in whatever was written there.

"That's what you were so concerned about? A notebook?"

She kept reading.

"Hey," he said, rounding a corner. "I'm risking my life to help you. You could at least give me a few answers."

"This notebook was in my brother's cabin. He'd hidden it there. Someplace special where he knew I'd find it."

"What's in it? A treasure map?"

"Notes from cases he was working. It doesn't seem to be anything out of the ordinary. A couple thefts, a domestic dispute, there's some witnesses listed with phone numbers, and—"

"Your brother's a police officer?"

"Yes."

Logan's gut clenched. He chose his next words carefully. "Where is your brother now?"

A couple of blinks but no answer—instead she continued reading. An awkward silence settled over the conversation, and he waited to see if she would say more.

She finally took a deep breath and shut the notebook. "They told me that he was shot in the line of duty." Her voice was barely a whisper. "But I don't believe them."

"You don't?"

"No. He'd called me the day before he died and left a message. He mentioned a cold case he was working, and that things were out of control. He seemed...I don't know...

like he was scared of something or someone. The next thing I knew, he was dead."

"I'm so sorry."

"It's devastated our parents. Especially my mother. She'll never be the same."

She tightened her grip on the notebook in her lap and turned toward the window. Quiet now, lost in her own thoughts, while he tried to control his. How could this be?

He gripped the wheel, sweat pricking his hairline. He'd met her brother. He was the doctor on shift the day the officer was brought into the emergency room. A gunshot wound, a bad one, which was rare in River Falls, where most of the emergencies involved either blunt trauma or hiking injuries. He'd done what he could, but the truth was, if there'd been a more experienced doctor, no, a *different* doctor, in the ER that night, her brother might still be alive. And now here he was, looking directly at the pain his failure had caused. Was this God's way of punishing him? Of telling him that he wasn't meant to be a doctor?

Emma focused on the bucolic scene out the window. Farmhouses and whitewashed fences, slanted barns and corralled horses whizzed by at the same pace that worried thoughts raced through her mind. Those cameras in the cabin… Someone had been watching and waiting for her to arrive and find the notebook. Who? And why? What was it about this notebook? She'd expected to find more in the special hiding place in the cabin, but this was it. How could that be?

Safe and away from the danger for now, her muscles loosened, and her eyes grew heavy. She allowed herself to drift into sleep until she felt the truck come to a stop. She stirred and sat up, trying to get her bearings. They were in a parking lot next to a squat brick building with green awnings. The only other car, a blue, older-model Honda Accord, was in the space next to them.

Logan turned off the engine. "We're in River Falls at a medical clinic. I want you to get checked out, especially that gash in your shoulder, in case you need stitches."

He got out and came around to her side, helping her out of the passenger seat. Her hair was matted against her head, her clothing torn and rumpled, and she reeked of river water and wood smoke. She didn't want to be here. What she wanted was food and water and a hot shower, but she agreed to the care and followed him with heavy, cumbersome legs. Halfway across the lot, she faltered.

"I've got you," he said, placing a steady hand on her elbow. He continued to help her as they made their way to the back door, where a woman in scrubs greeted them. She was probably in her thirties, with a neat dark bun, strong jaw, soft brown eyes and a wide-band watch strapped to her wrist. Logan introduced her as Rachel, and she took charge, leading Emma into a small room, where she checked her vitals and jotted down a few notes before turning her attention to the wound. She peeled back the bandage.

Emma cringed and let out a little gasp.

Rachel eyed her. "Sorry. I know that hurts. How are you holding up?"

"It's okay. I'm fine." But Emma's stomach reeled at the sight of her own raw, inflamed flesh.

Rachel snatched a small paper cup from a dispenser and filled it with water. "Here. Take a couple sips."

Emma gulped the water down and crumpled the cup in her hand, turning her head and closing her eyes. Metal instruments clanked on the bedside tray. Rachel's gloved hand felt cold against her skin.

"How'd you get this cut?" Rachel asked.

"Floated the river without a raft."

"Ouch! Could be a lot worse, then. You're lucky you ran into a doctor out there in the woods."

Emma's eyes popped open. "Doctor?"

"He didn't tell you?" Rachel shook her head and smiled. "Sounds like Logan. Or should I say, Dr. Greer. Although I never call him that. Don't have to. I'm his sister. Older sister, but just by a couple years."

"He's your brother?"

"That's right. I'm going to cleanse this. Hold tight."

Emma flinched and drew a sharp breath.

"It's not as bad as it feels, I promise," Rachel assured her. "Just a few sutures, and then you'll be ready to go."

"Are you a doctor, too?"

"A physician's assistant."

"Can't be easy working for your brother."

She laughed, her brown eyes sparkling. She had an easy way about her.

"It's not. And the pay is lousy. I only work here because I believe in what he's doing."

Emma glanced around. The room was simple, but well equipped. From what she'd seen of the outside, it wasn't very big. "What exactly *is* he doing?"

"We're in one of the poorest counties in West Virginia. Sure, we've got a hospital and other doctors in the area, but most folks don't have health care insurance. In fact, half the folks around here don't have enough food on the table. So, for everyday doctoring, those who can't afford the other facilities come here. Logan staffs the place with me and a few volunteers, and most of the equipment and stuff he gets through donations."

"How does he afford to keep the place open?"

"We had a donor to start, got some grants, too, but he works a few shifts a week in the ER. He saves money by living in our family home and puts most of his income into keeping this place going." She shrugged. "What can I say? My brother's a pretty cool guy."

Emma forced a smile. Her own brother had been a cool guy, too. Strong and faithful, yet God chose to let him die. She cleared her throat and blinked back tears. *Stay focused*, she told herself. There was nothing she could do to bring Daniel back. Nothing. But she could—and would—find out who'd killed him and why. Then she'd bring his killer to justice.

THREE

Logan waited in his office, sifting mindlessly through paperwork, while his thoughts centered on Emma, her brother's death and the man intent on harming her. Whatever her brother investigated had posed a threat to someone. At least that was what Emma had led him to believe. What did he really know about her or the situation? He hadn't even known her last name until she filled out her medical forms. And how did he fit into any of this? Besides the fact that he was partially responsible for her brother's death and—

"All done." Rachel's voice interrupted his thoughts. She stood in the doorway, Emma next to her. She had more color in her cheeks and was sipping from a small bottle of apple juice that Rachel must have given her.

"Good. How's the patient?"

Emma smiled briefly. "Okay, considering everything. I'm so grateful for your help." She looked at Rachel. "And yours, too."

He drew in a deep breath. He wasn't going to let her fend for herself. Not with that man still out there. "What are your plans from here?"

"I don't know. My Jeep is still up at the trailhead by my brother's cabin. I have to find a way to go back and get it, or—"

"I don't think that's a good idea." Logan stood and walked over. "It'll be dark soon. First thing tomorrow morning I'll go up with my brother-in-law and get it for you. If you're okay with that. I don't want to chance that you run into that man again."

Emma tensed and shot Rachel a look.

Rachel raised a brow. "Logan already told me that someone was after you out there in the woods."

"I didn't tell her everything, but you can trust Rachel. And me. You're going to have to trust someone. You could still be in danger."

"You should talk to the sheriff," Rachel said. "This is serious. Who knows what type of dangerous person he is, or who he'll go after next?"

"I...I don't think that's a good idea."

Logan frowned. "But that man shot at you. He tried to kill you."

"I don't want to bring the sheriff into it, not yet." Emma capped her juice and picked at the bottle label. "He was after me for a reason. I think it has something to do with a case Daniel was investigating. I'm not sure who it involved or who I can trust."

Meaning the cops, Logan thought.

Rachel narrowed her eyes. "Who's Daniel?"

"My brother."

Logan watched as Emma shrank into herself. This discussion was too much for her, especially after everything she'd been through today. "We can talk about all of this later," he told Rachel. "For now, let's figure out a place for Emma to stay tonight. She needs somewhere safe to rest and recuperate."

"Okay...well, that's easy. She can stay at our place." Rachel pulled her phone from her pocket and stepped down the hall. "I'll just call and let Joe know."

Emma protested, but Rachel waved her off and ducked into the examination room, phone to her ear.

"Don't worry," Logan told her. "Joe's a great guy. And you'll feel better once you get some hot food and a good night's sleep."

Her expression turned dark. "I doubt that."

"What do you mean?"

"My brother was murdered. I'm sure of it. And the only thing that is going to make me feel better is finding his killer and making him pay for what he's done."

The vehemence in her voice shocked him, and her words, now hanging bitter and angry in the air between them, seemed to spring out of a deep darkness. He understood that darkness. He'd faced it before in his own life. And without God, it would have consumed him.

Normally, staying overnight in a stranger's house would have been awkward, but Rachel and Joe were so warm and inviting, Emma felt like she'd known them her whole life.

Their quaint two-story farmhouse—the original Greer family home, Rachel told her—had faded and warped over the years, now showing a slanted wraparound porch, worn hardwood floors and crumbling plaster walls. The kitchen was the only updated room. It looked like it'd just been the feature of a DIY home show.

"A total renovation," Rachel was saying. "But so worth it, don't you think? I mean, the kitchen is the heart of the home, right?"

Emma nodded and dragged another corn chip through salsa. Her hair was still damp from a shower, leaving wet spots on the sweatshirt Rachel had loaned her. Logan stood next to her, leaning against the granite counter, watching Joe mix a dressing for the salad.

"Hope you're hungry," Joe said.

"Starved," Emma replied.

"Then you've come to the right place." Rachel hugged her hubby from behind, nuzzling her head against his shoulder. "Joe microwaves frozen lasagna with the best of them."

"Hey, now. No giving away my secrets."

Store-bought or not, the lasagna was amazing. Steaming hot, cheesy and comforting. Very comforting, Emma decided, and so was the company. The four of them ate and talked and joked as if they'd been friends for years. They asked her about DC and her work as an investigative journalist, and she even told them about a recent award she'd received for an exposé of Victor Duran, a big-time drug trafficker. Then, realizing it sounded like bragging, she tried to brush it off as not a big deal. But she'd noticed how Logan listened intently and seemed impressed, and that pleased her.

Things were going so well that she almost felt like her old self, before Daniel's murder, when her life was carefree and she'd spent many evenings like this, hanging out with friends, eating and chatting. Then Joe broke the spell with, "Logan told us about your brother. And I'm sorry. I think I may have met him once."

"You met Daniel?" Emma reached for her water and took a shaky sip.

"He pulled me over out on Route 41, where it runs by Cheaters Fork, that straightaway part. You all know how easy it is to get speeding out there." He looked at Logan. "I remember you getting pulled over at the same spot."

Logan's hand flew up. "We're talking about you, buddy. Not me."

Joe chuckled and continued. "Did your brother have red hair like yours?"

Emma nodded. "We're twins."

"Twins? Yeah, I can see that now. Anyway, he gave me a speeding ticket, but we got talking a bit and I could tell he was a good guy. Not that I was able to talk him out of the ticket, but he reminded me that a ticket was better than being dea—"

The table fell silent.

Joe flushed red. "I'm sorry. I wasn't thinking."

"No. That's okay. Really. That sounds like something my brother would say." Emma swallowed hard, trying to keep it together. "I remember he was thrilled to get this job. We vacationed here when we were young. My dad worked overtime and saved enough to buy that parcel of land where the cabin sits. He and Daniel built it together. Well, I helped, too." The memory made her both happy and sad. "Anyway, it was always Daniel's dream to move here." *But someone cut that dream short.* Her jaw tightened. It surprised her how quickly she became angry these days.

She took a deep breath, unclenched her fist and pulled the notebook from her pocket. "I need help with something. I believe that the man who shot at us was after this, but I can't figure out why. There must be something important in it. Daniel had hidden it in a secret spot that only he and I knew about. Since you all have lived here your whole lives, I thought maybe you might see something I've missed." She passed it across the table to Logan. Rachel and Joe moved closer, looking over his shoulder.

"The first entry is dated just a few weeks before Daniel was killed," Emma explained. "There are a lot of case notes in here. It all looks like regular police stuff to me. Except toward the end, where he made a note to himself." She pointed it out: *Get Pruitt's permission to reopen case.*

"Pruitt is the sheriff," Logan said. "Has been for a long time."

Daniel's memorial service was back home, and a lot of his police family made the trip to attend, but Emma didn't remember meeting the sheriff. It was all a blur, though.

"Sounds like your brother wanted to reopen a cold case," Logan said, flipping back through the pages. "Most of the rest of this looks like normal police work. There's no other mention of the case or anything that stands out."

Emma nodded. "Yeah. There's got to be more to it. He left a voicemail message right before he died. He said he was at the cabin and mentioned the case he was working on. He told me that he didn't know who he could trust and that he'd hidden something. I assumed that he'd hidden proof about the cold case at the cabin, but this was all I found." She rubbed her temples and blinked. "I must be missing something."

Rachel reached over and touched her arm. "Maybe things will be clearer after some rest."

"You're right. I'm so tired, I can't think straight." She pushed back from the table and grabbed her plate. "I'll help you get these dishes done."

Rachel popped up and grabbed the plate. "No, you won't. Go on to bed. I'll take care of the kitchen."

Logan handed back the notebook. "And Joe and I will get your car first thing. Probably before you're awake. Do you have the keys?"

"Upstairs in my pack."

He followed her upstairs to the bedroom where she was staying. She glanced around the room as she rummaged through the pack for the keys. "Do Rachel and Joe have children?"

"No. Why?"

"All these horse posters. Was this Rachel's room when she was a kid?"

"Oh." He shifted and cleared his throat. "Uh...this wasn't Rachel's room. It was Kate's. Our youngest sister."

Something told her not to ask, but curiosity got the best of her. "You didn't mention Kate earlier. Does she live here in town?" She held out the keys. His hand trembled as he reached for them. "Logan, what is it? Did I say something wrong?"

"No, not at all. It's just that...Kate disappeared when she was a teenager. We don't know what happened to her."

Emma gasped, her hand darting to his arm. "Oh, Logan. I'm so sorry."

He stepped back and looked at the floor. "It's okay. Really. It's been a long time."

"It must be so difficult." She ducked her chin, trying to slide under his gaze. "I can't imagine not knowing." His shoulders rounded and he cleared his throat, and when he finally looked at her, his eyes were wet with tears. "Are you okay?" she asked. "Do you want to talk about it?"

"No." He turned and headed for the door. "I'm fine. Good night, Emma. I'll see you in the morning."

Emma stared after him, her heart breaking for Logan and his family. She began moving about the room, trying to imagine the teen who once lived here. A young woman who loved horses, read sweet romance novels and still kept a teddy bear on her bed. What were her dreams? And why did God allow such horrible things to happen to innocent people?

Like Daniel.

Hot anger swelled inside her, and a flash of light drew her to the window. She brushed aside lacy pink curtains and leaned close to the pane. Across the street, headlights clicked off and an interior dome light of a small sports car briefly flicked on, illuminating the outline of a man.

She flinched, jumped away from the window and pressed her back to the wall. Her anger turned to cold fear that the man from the woods had followed her, planned to kill her, maybe Rachel and Joe and Logan, too. A shiver ran along her spine. *Stop it, Emma! This is silly. Think...* She shook her head, chiding herself. No, the man in the woods was thin and wiry, and looked nothing like the round profile she'd just glimpsed. *I'm tired, that's all. Seeing killers around every corner.*

Drawing in a deep breath, she faced the window again and pressed her forehead against the pane. No movement inside the car. Nothing. Just another vehicle parked by the curb, its driver probably one of the nearby neighbors. She turned away from the window, went to sleep in a pink-covered bed and dreamed of Daniel and horses and a missing girl.

"She asked about Kate." Logan had swept the glass out of his truck early the next morning and patched the back window with cardboard and duct tape. Not the best look, but it'd done the trick. Now he kept his eyes on the road as he drove and talked to Joe. Rain threatened, and the wind had picked up, making it hard to steer. The moments right before sunrise were dangerous in the mountains, especially this time of year, when deer were on the run from hunters.

"Oh, yeah? What'd you tell her?"

Logan shrugged. "Not much. Just that she's our sister. And that she's missing."

Joe nodded and sipped his coffee. They'd stopped off at the gas station before leaving town and were on their way to get Emma's Jeep. Daniel's Jeep, actually. Emma told Logan that she'd flown from DC and took a cab to the sheriff's department, where Daniel's Jeep was still parked. Driving it, she said, made her feel close to him. He got that. For months after Kate's disappearance, he'd kept one of her favorite sweatshirts. Still had it, in fact. At first, it smelled like her: the outdoors, horses and Daisy perfume. He remembered the first time he realized the smell had faded, that it'd upset him—

"Did you hear me, buddy?" Joe's voice interrupted his thoughts.

Logan blinked. "What's that?"

"I was asking if you planned to tell Emma the rest of the story about Kate."

He'd been asking himself the same question. The look on Emma's face when he told her about Kate, and the touch of her hand and her concern about him, it all seemed genuine. But what would she think if she knew the truth about Kate? Emma barely knew him and his family, didn't know their history or the history of the town. All she knew was that her brother had died serving the people here. And now she was also in danger, being hunted down by an armed man in the woods.

Truth was, he'd held back from telling her more about Kate because he was afraid that she might think the worst, like most of the people around here. Not that her opinion should matter to him. His father had taught him not to worry about what others thought, only what God thought. That very thought had carried him through many rough spots, especially since his return to River Falls. But the truth was, he did care what Emma thought of—

"The turnoff!"

Logan cranked the wheel and took a hard right onto the next road. "Sorry about that."

Joe swiped at his clothes. "Oh, man. You made me spill my coffee. All over my work pants, too." Joe had been at the mine before it closed. He'd taken a temporary job since then. Currently he was working maintenance at the hospital. "What's wrong with you this morning, anyway? Don't answer that. I already know."

Logan was focused on the road again. "Know what?"

"Oh, come on," Joe laughed. "You know what I'm talking about. You like Emma, and it's messing with your mind. Making you all love crazy. I get it. I've been there."

"*Been* there? Aren't you still there? Or is there something I should be telling my sister?"

"The trailhead's just another mile up the road," Joe said. "Just so you don't miss it. And no, I'm not all love crazy with your sister anymore."

"You're not?"

"No. That's for rookies. I'm deeply, madly in love with your sister, and it gets better every day."

A strange mix of happiness and envy hit Logan. "I want that one day."

He surprised himself. Ever since Kate went missing, he'd spent his time keeping busy. Really busy. The army, med school, his clinic... None of that left a lot of time for dating. Not that he'd even thought much about a relationship. Not until now.

Joe slapped him on the shoulder. "I hope you get it, buddy. I really do." He pointed up the road. "There's our turn. Let's just ease around this next corner, okay?"

Logan pulled into the trailhead parking lot and rolled to a stop. Across the lot, a gray Jeep Wrangler with chrome accents was parked at a slant, with the top off and mud splattered on the wheel wells. Just as Emma had described it. "This is it. I've got the keys," he said. "I'll follow you back."

He approached the Jeep, the keys jangling between his fingers and a stiff wind whipping his hair. *Cool vehicle*, he thought, gripping the door handle, but the open top was going to make for a breezy drive home. He started to open the door and then froze, raising his hands and stepping backward.

Inside, a small wire ran from the door, under the side of the steering column, to the pin of a grenade.

"What's wrong?" Joe called from behind.

"Get out of here! Booby trap!"

The wind caught the partially opened door and forced it back on its hinges. Logan turned, dived and hit the pavement just as the Jeep exploded, raining metal shards around him.

"He works too hard. That's his problem," Rachel was telling her.

Emma listened intently, surprised that she was so interested in hearing about Logan. They'd just met, but already she sensed there was something special about him.

Rachel continued, "I had to force him to take some time off. He's so stubborn. But just think what would have happened if I hadn't pushed it. You might not be here, that's what."

Emma nodded. Rachel was right about that.

"How's that shoulder of yours feeling, by the way?"

Emma shrugged. "Sore. But better, I think." The residual pain was a constant reminder of her harrowing experience in the woods. She tried to put that memory behind her and enjoy the moment. Rachel was a hoot, and Emma loved sitting at her table, sipping coffee and chatting like old friends.

So far, Emma had heard about Rachel and Logan's father, who'd worked his whole life mining coal and died when they were still in high school. And their mother, the strongest woman Rachel had ever known, who had gone on to raise the kids single-handedly while running a successful at-home day care, right in this house, working every single day except Sundays right up to the moment she passed. And now Rachel had moved on to talking about Logan and his chance encounter with Emma.

"Providence. That's what it was," Rachel concluded.

"Providence?"

Rachel leaned forward. "Why, yes. Providence. You don't think it was just a coincidence—do ya?—that Logan happened to be at that very spot, in the middle of the woods, his fishing line getting tangled up just inches from where you were lying, hurt and afraid."

"Well, when you put it that way…"

"What other way is there to put it? Don't you see, Emma? God put him there at that moment for a reason. And that reason was to meet you. You don't have to believe it if you don't want to, but I know it's the truth." Rachel finished her coffee and pushed back from the table. She carried her empty mug to the sink. Emma started to ask about the sports car parked outside last night, but hesitated. Rachel seemed in a hurry.

"I'm off to work," she said. "Wednesday's our busiest day of the week, and I'm flying solo while Logan's on vacation. But the guys should be back any minute. I'll make sure all the doors are locked on my way out. Will you be okay here until they get back?"

"Sure. And once I get my Jeep, I'll go into town and pick up some clothes so I can give these back to you."

Rachel headed for the door. "Don't worry about the

jeans. I can't get into them anymore, and the way things are going, I might not for some time, if ever. They're yours if you want them."

Emma's gaze automatically slid to Rachel's midsection. It was hard to tell with her scrubs, but Emma had to wonder if Rachel didn't just hint at a little secret of her own.

As soon as Rachel left, Emma poured another cup of coffee and carried it to the living room, settled in the recliner and pulled a throw blanket over her lap. She'd borrowed Rachel's laptop to do a quick check of her work email and found two emails from news outlets requesting spin-off articles from her exposé on Victor Duran. She ignored those and clicked over to a search engine, eager to research some of the dates and names in Daniel's notebook. What had Daniel stumbled into? She typed in a few of the names scribbled in the notebook: a suspect mentioned in connection with a car theft, a couple of names connected with a domestic dispute call, and the last two names, witnesses to a fatal accident on Route 41 involving a speeding car. She thought of Joe's speeding ticket story last night, and Daniel's advice to him. It was so like Daniel to try to be helpful, not just do his job. She started to spiral into grief again. She swallowed back a lump in her throat and refocused. There'd be time to cry later. Now she needed to find answers.

But there was nothing. Only the usual social media references, property tax records and other small things. Nothing that linked to any old crimes or looked like a motive for killing her brother. She gave up and closed her eyes for a moment. *A nap would be a good thing.* She'd hardly slept the night before, in a strange bed, with a sore shoulder and a thousand worries running through her mind.

She'd just set the laptop aside and tugged the blanket up to her chin when the neighbor's dog started barking. And barking. The poor thing was all worked up. She tuned out the noise and returned to nap mode, but a funny feeling crept over her.

If it feels wrong, it usually is. Her mother's words, and advice that'd served Emma well over the years.

She got up and crossed to the front window, peering through the sheer curtains. The dog next door was going wild, jumping against the fence, snarling and chomping at the air, all the time looking toward Rachel and Joe's house. What did he see? Emma scanned the yard again, saw nothing, and was about to turn away when she spied movement in the hedge along the far side of the property. She leaned closer to the window, squinted and waited, her heart rate kicking up. Was it the thin man from the woods? *No. No way. This is silly.* Just like last night, her mind was tired and playing tricks on her. *Get a grip, Emma.* She headed back to the chair, then stopped when she heard glass shattering in the kitchen.

She spiraled into a panic. Someone was breaking into the house.

Get out, she thought, but the dog barking, the movement in the hedges... Were there two attackers? She couldn't make a run for it, and there was no house phone, and her cell was destroyed in the river. There was no way to call for help. She wheeled, snatched the fireplace poker and ran up the stairs and into the bedroom she'd slept in last night. The closet. She darted inside, crouching behind hanging clothes and plastic storage bins.

Her legs cramped, and her breath shallowed as she inhaled the smell of musty wool and fear-soured body odor.

Hers. She tightened her sweat-slicked palms around the poker, her pulse pounding in her ears. *God, help me. If he comes near me, I'll kill him.*

FOUR

"Something's not right," Logan said as soon as they walked through the front door of Joe's house.

His ears still rang from the explosion. His jeans were torn, palms and knees embedded with pieces of asphalt, and nerves on edge. The explosion brought back wartime trauma and propelled him into hypervigilance. As soon as he saw the laptop turned over on the floor and a blanket crumpled next to it, he knew something had happened.

He was about to call out for Emma when he heard a sound at the rear of the house. He ran to the kitchen, Joe on his heels, as a man dashed out the back door.

"Check the house," Joe ordered as he sprinted off in pursuit of the man.

Logan snatched a knife from the kitchen drawer and moved through the first floor, checking every room and every hiding spot as he called out for Rachel and Emma. No response. Fear and dread surged through him. He took a couple of deep breaths, trying to calm himself. They had to be okay.

"Rachel. Emma!"

"Up here."

He whipped around and scaled the stairs, then found Emma in Kate's bedroom by the closet with a fireplace poker in her hand. Her face was pale and her eyes wide with fear. She looked small and vulnerable, and he fought back an urge to pull her close and comfort her.

The poker shook in her hands. "Someone was after me. They broke into the house."

He grabbed her shoulders. "You're okay now. Where's Rachel?"

"She went to work and…I heard glass breaking, so I ran up here and hid in the closet. I don't have my phone. I couldn't call the police."

He gently took the poker from her. "You did the right thing. Come on, let's get out of here."

He led her downstairs. Joe was hunched, doubled over in the family room, out of breath. "I lost him." He glanced up and straightened, his face paling. "Where's Rachel? Where's my wife?"

"It's okay, buddy. She's fine. She left for work before the guy broke in. Emma's all right. She hid in the closet."

He took another deep breath and exhaled. "I was on him until he ran into those trees behind the house. Not sure which way he went."

"There might have been two of them. I thought I'd seen someone in the hedge just before the glass in the kitchen door was smashed."

Joe looked at Emma. "Did you get a look at them?"

She wrapped her arms around herself. "No. I'm sorry. I was so scared. I just ran upstairs and hid. Didn't see anything."

"It's okay. I'm just glad you're not hurt. I'm going to call Rachel, so she's aware. Then I'll check the damage to the back door, and we'll figure out what to do from there."

As soon as Joe left, Emma turned to Logan. "How did

they know to find me here? Are they following me? Watching me?"

"They must have followed us. We didn't tell anyone you were here," Logan said.

"But why? I don't know anything. What do they want? The notebook? There's nothing in it."

"But whoever is after you doesn't know that."

She shook her head. "I need to figure out what cold case Daniel was working on."

Logan agreed, then hesitated, not quite knowing how to relay the next bit of news. "Joe and I went out to Daniel's cabin. The Jeep is gone, Emma. I'm sorry."

"Gone? Someone stole it?"

"No. It…blew up."

"What?"

"It was rigged to explode when the door opened."

Her expression hardened as she eyed the scrapes on his hands and knees and his torn jeans. "You mean it exploded while you were there?"

"I saw the trip wire before—"

"You could have been killed."

"I wasn't. I'm okay. And I'm right here."

Emma tightened her arms around her midsection, tears stinging her eyes. "I can't believe this is happening. I shouldn't have dragged you two into this."

"We're here because something very bad is going on. And we want to help you." Again, he thought about comforting her, pulling her close, but he didn't cross that line. "I know the Jeep belonged to your brother, and I'm so sorry. We reported it to the sheriff's department. They asked for your contact information, since you're the owner. I didn't know your number and, well, your phone is broken anyway, so I gave them my number. They'll be in touch soon."

"Whoever did this won't stop until they've eradicated whatever it is that Daniel discovered." She pulled the notebook from her pocket and clutched it in her hand. "I need to make a copy of this and put the original somewhere safe."

Logan agreed. "We can do that at the clinic. We have a copier in the office there. Then you should go back home, Emma. Your parents need you right now, and it'd be safer for you there."

"What my family needs is the truth behind Daniel's murder. If my parents have any hope for peace, they at least deserve to know why he was killed."

"Maybe you're right, but I think we need to bring the sheriff into this. I know you don't trust him, but—"

"No, I don't. What if Daniel uncovered corruption at the sheriff's office? You saw his notation. He was going to ask to have a cold case reopened. We don't know if he got around to that or not. But if he did and the sheriff was afraid that something was going to get out—"

"I've known Pruitt all my life. He's as straight as they come. But you're right—there could be a connection, maybe someone close to the sheriff." He raked his hand through his hair. "Okay, let's wait on the sheriff as long as we can. He'll have questions about the Jeep, though. And we can't lie to him."

"No. What's there to lie about? We have no solid proof that the explosion is connected to Daniel's investigation into the cold case. Or if today wasn't just an ordinary burglary. It's just a hunch at this point. If I do get something solid, I'll take it straight to the authorities." Emma opened the notebook. "I started researching the names that are in here. There's not much online, so I'm going to look into some of these people on my own. I just need to find somewhere else to stay and get to a car rental place, so I can pick up something to drive."

"This is River Falls. We don't have a car rental office. The nearest place to pick up a rental is about a hundred and twenty miles from here."

She stood and started pacing. "I'll get something figured out. I'll need to get a new phone and laptop. I can't keep borrowing Rachel's. And I need clothes."

Logan smiled. The small and vulnerable Emma he'd found trembling with a fireplace poker now appeared wiry and single-minded as she allowed her thoughts to tumble out.

He admired her determination and understood her need to help her family find answers. He'd spent years searching for Kate when she went missing, never finding a single lead. Maybe Emma wouldn't find the answers she wanted, either. But in Emma's situation, someone had not only killed her brother but was after her now. He wanted to help her. But more than that, he wanted to protect her. Nothing could bring Kate back, but he would not let Emma be another innocent victim. "Let me take you around to see these people."

"No. Not after today. I wouldn't forgive myself if either of you were hurt. This is my problem, not yours." She picked the laptop off the floor, looked it over and carefully slid it onto the coffee table. "And what about your work? I don't want to take you away from your patients."

"Technically, I'm still on vacation, so I don't have any responsibilities for the next few days."

"No, I really can't ask—"

"You didn't ask. I'm volunteering." There was no way he was going to sit back and allow her to go at this alone. "You were targeted here, in my family home, so I have a vested interest in helping you find this person. We can run a few errands first, get some of the stuff you need, and then stop by the clinic to make copies of the notebook. After that, we'll start checking into some of your leads."

She breathed out a sigh of relief. "Okay. Thank you, Logan."

They picked up supplies and got back on the road. Emma rode in silence as she fought back worries that zipped through her mind: getting the remains of the Jeep towed; if Daniel's insurance would still cover it; what she was going to drive. Thoughts that tried, and failed, to eclipse the shocking reality: someone had tried to kill her.

The first address led them to a small ranch-style house on the west side of River Falls with peeling paint and corroded aluminum window frames. Emma double-checked the house number.

"This is it. Thanks again for helping me." She pointed at the copies of the notebook they'd made, now in a folder on the floorboard of his car. They'd also stopped by the electronics store and purchased a new laptop and phone, and she'd spent a little time setting up her apps and sending her new phone number to her parents and close friends. "And for being here with me," she added, looking at the dilapidated house. Curtains hung limp inside the windows, with no lights poking through. The steps sagged, and the weedy yard showed no hint of recent activity. The house appeared abandoned or at least neglected. "I wouldn't want to be here, interviewing Crawford on my own." Especially in this neighborhood, she thought. But she kept it to herself. She didn't have it much better growing up and remembered how it hurt when people judged her for what she didn't have. She glanced over her shoulder. "Are you sure no one's followed us?"

Logan checked the mirrors one more time and reached for the car door handle. "I haven't seen anything. Let's go and get this over with."

They made their way up the walk. Emma knocked on the door. The front window curtain stirred. She waited, wondering what was taking Crawford so long, then heard a noise coming from the back of the house.

Logan heard it, too, and motioned for her to follow him. They pushed through a path edged in a row of overgrown hedges just as a man slid out the back door.

"Excuse me!" she called out.

He startled and turned to her, his expression a mixture of fear and anger. He looked like he was going to bolt, but instead he crammed his hands into his pockets and shot her an insolent glance.

"Jake Crawford?" Logan asked, stepping forward.

Crawford was probably in his twenties but looked much older, with deep horizontal lines etched under a receding hairline. His cheeks were shallow and his arms bone thin. His stained T-shirt strained over his midsection.

"Leave me alone," he said, his words slightly slurred.

"We just want to talk," Emma said. "A few questions, that's all."

"I told them on the phone that I ain't got the money right now."

"This isn't about money. It's about Officer Hayes. Daniel Hayes."

Crawford's eyes darted between her and Logan. "That cop? What about him? Did he tell you we talked?" Emma started to explain, but Crawford interrupted. "He wasn't supposed to say nothin'. Told me he'd keep my name out of things. But I knew he'd tell. All cops are liars."

Emma took a small step forward. "Daniel didn't lie to you, Jake. He didn't tell me about you. I found you another way."

"Whatever. Look, I gave him everything I knew already. I'm supposed to be in the clear. We had a deal. Just ask him."

Logan spoke up. "We need a little more information and then we'll leave."

"I told him I don't know nothing more. He needs to talk to Mink."

Logan tensed. "Michael Kincaid?"

Crawford nodded. "Yeah. That's right. Mink. I told that cop everything I knew about that night. I came clean about Mink, too. Told him that Mink couldn't have done it because he was with me."

Emma was confused. "Couldn't have done what? What was Officer Hayes questioning you about?"

Crawford's gaze focused on Emma. His eyes widened. "Who are you? You look like—"

Crack!

Emma ducked and clutched her head, her ears ringing. Instantly, she dived to the ground, her face forward, the wormy taste of dirt and wet leaves assaulting her tongue. Logan landed next to her. He reached out and slid his arm protectively across her back. She turned her head and saw Jake's body a few feet away, sprawled on his stomach, blood pooling around his midsection. Panic surged through her. "He's been shot. Crawford's shot. He's bleeding."

Another bullet ripped through the dirt only inches from her head, kicking up dust and making her shudder.

"Stay down!" Logan hissed. And she did. He held her tight, and everything grew silent except for their breathing. When would the next shot come? Would it hit Logan? Or her? And was Crawford dead?

An engine revved to life, followed by the sound of tires on asphalt, and she felt Logan's body relax a little. He stood and grabbed his jacket, pointing toward the house. "Inside, Emma. Get inside and stay there."

Her breath came in short bursts as she bolted inside and crouched with her back against the mudroom wall. A high-pitched buzz filled her brain. She gritted her teeth, but her body shook uncontrollably. She waited and waited, until she couldn't stand it anymore, and then she edged toward the door and peered around the corner.

"Is he alive?"

"Barely. I called 911. Help's coming." Sweat poured down the sides of Logan's face, and she noticed a tremor in his hands as he pressed his jacket against Crawford's wound. Something was off. His movements were slow and forced—even though he was a doctor, he seemed confused, like his mind was somewhere else.

"Logan, are you okay?"

His head snapped up. His features turned angry. "I told you to get back inside."

Emma flinched, hurt by his outburst, but she couldn't look away, so she continued to watch as Crawford writhed in pain, anguished moans escaping his quivering lips. She could hardly believe that she was just talking to this man and now he'd been shot and was fighting for his life. She should pray, and the old Emma would have prayed for Crawford, that God would heal him if it was His will, but that was before God betrayed her, betrayed Daniel. She tried, but anger stood in the way of the words.

Finally, the sirens sounded directly out front. An ambulance and two cop cars with deputies arrived. The officers secured the area, firing off questions, as the paramedics tended to the victim. Emma was shuffled to one of the police cruisers and placed in the back seat. She watched as police and paramedics came and went.

After a few minutes, a deputy sheriff approached. She opened the cruiser door and looked at Emma's torn shirt and blood-pricked palms. "You doing okay, ma'am?"

Emma nodded.

"I'll have a medic look you over in a minute."

"I'm fine. Is Crawford...?"

"I don't know. I'm Deputy Davis. I need to get a statement from you, okay?" She took out a pen and notebook, identical to the notebook Emma had in her coat pocket, the one that belonged to Daniel, and her heart sank.

The deputy was about her age, with long hair pulled back and woven into a neat bun at the nape of her neck. She was full-figured with ample curves and soft folds of flawless skin edging her jaw. Her dark eyes were sharp and intense by comparison. *She's probably a tough cop*, Emma thought, then stopped herself. Her attention to detail worked well in her career interviewing subjects, but it made her overanalyze people and make assumptions that were often incorrect.

The deputy started with the basics, wanting Emma's name and address. She looked up from her notebook when Emma said her full name. "Hayes? Daniel Hayes's sister?" Her eyes softened. "I'm sorry. I should have known. You look like him."

Emma nodded.

Deputy Davis shifted her stance. "What are you doing here at this house? This guy's got a record. He was arrested not too long ago."

Emma couldn't lie, but she couldn't tell her everything,

either. Out of the corner of her eye, she saw Crawford being transported to the ambulance. Logan followed, giving instructions to the medics. Emma peeled her gaze away and forced her full attention back to Davis's questions. "I came here to talk to Crawford. I thought he might know something about my brother's death."

"What's Crawford have to do with your brother's death? Danny was killed during a traffic stop. Every cop in the county is looking for the guy who did it."

Danny. Emma used to call her brother by that nickname all the time. The memory sent waves of sadness through her.

"Ms. Hayes, what made you think that Crawford knows anything about Danny's death?" Davis asked again.

"I can't really say." Emma swiped her sweaty palms on her jeans, surprised by the bloody streaks they left on the fabric, but she didn't look up, didn't meet Deputy Davis's gaze. She wouldn't say anything else, not until she knew who she could trust.

Davis sighed, stepped aside and spoke into her radio for a few seconds, then returned. She'd put away her notebook and pen and bent down until she was face-to-face with Emma. "Listen, I'm sorry for what you're going through. But I think you know something that could help us here. You can trust me. I knew Danny well. We, uh…we—"

"Emma, are you okay?" Logan appeared at her side, bent down and scooped up her hands. "You've skinned your palms."

His hands felt good on hers, but she still pulled them back. "Thanks to you, I'm alive. How is Crawford? Is he going to be okay?"

Logan rubbed the back of his neck. "It doesn't look good. He's already lost a lot of blood."

Another sheriff's vehicle drove up, and Pruitt clamored out of the passenger side. Deputy Davis excused herself to talk to him and a couple of other deputies. They huddled, exchanging notes, shooting an occasional glance Emma's way.

"Did they question you?" she asked Logan.

"Yes, and I told him everything I knew."

"About the notebook, too?"

"Had to, Emma. Didn't have much choice. This is a man's life." He shook his head. "It doesn't look good for Crawford. He may die. We can't hold back any evidence."

"No, I know. This never would have happened if it weren't for me. The shooter must have been aiming for me and missed." Tears threatened Emma's eyes. "If I hadn't come here—"

"You couldn't have anticipated this. No one could have. And think about it. There were two shots fired. I don't think the shooter missed. I think the first bullet was intended for Crawford and the second was aimed for you. We've got to be more careful going forward. Whoever did this wanted to silence Crawford. He also must know or suspect we have Daniel's notebook, and he'll be watching us." He paused, then said, "Pruitt's looking over here. He's going to want the notebook."

She nodded. She should have gone to the sheriff earlier and turned it over. Maybe Crawford wouldn't be in an ambulance now. "When Crawford told us that name, Mink someone, you seemed to recognize it. Who is he?"

"Michael Kincaid. Mink is his nickname. Ten years ago, he killed a prominent man in our community and has been in prison ever since."

"Did you know the man he killed?"

"Knew of him, but we weren't friends or anything."

"So how did you know about—"

"Mink was my sister's boyfriend." Logan looked away, staring pensively at nothing. "He was dating her at the time she disappeared."

"Do you think he killed her, too?" Emma spoke gently. She may never be able to forgive God for taking her only brother from her, but she was able to have a funeral for him, bury him, experience a little closure. Not knowing what happened to someone so close to you would be torture.

Logan set his jaw. "I've thought so many different things over the years. Not that it matters what I think. There was money involved. Close to twenty thousand dollars that's never been found. To a couple of teens, that would have seemed like a fortune. There was also some evidence that Kate was with Mink as the murder went down. Public opinion is that she's gotten away with the money and eluded the authorities all these years, leaving Mink to take the rap."

Emma sat silent a moment. She'd assumed Kate had run away or been kidnapped, but the cause didn't matter, really. Regardless of the reason, Logan's family had been left with nothing but questions. "Evidence can be planted," Emma offered. As a journalist, she knew how easily people could be mistreated.

"My parents never for a minute believed that Kate was involved, and they never stopped looking for her. Never lost hope. Even Mom, all through her cancer, kept hope that if God didn't give her the answers now, He would in the next life."

Emma felt herself stiffen. She needed answers, too, but she didn't intend to wait on God to provide them.

Logan went on, "It's taken a long time to come to terms with it all. Even now, all these years later, I still struggle. I don't think I'll ever stop searching for Kate and the truth about what happened to her. That's why I can understand your need for answers about Daniel."

He stared straight into her eyes, and Emma saw that they both shared the same pain as well as a determination to learn the truth. Whatever that might be. Whatever it took.

FIVE

A couple of hours later, Logan entered the drive-through and picked up two bags of burgers. He stowed them on the back seat and glanced over at Emma. Her dark red hair was a tangled mess and her skin pale with smudges of dirt along the jawline, but she was still beautiful. *Beautiful.* How long had it been since he'd allowed himself to think of a woman that way? He'd dated a few women over the years, but every time the conversation turned to his sister, it was like a wall went up. Most women couldn't handle his troubled past, or worse, they thought Kate was guilty of murder. They judged her without even knowing her. But with Emma it was different. She'd judged her, too, not as someone who was guilty but instead as possibly innocent. Her words echoed in his mind: "Evidence can be planted." She'd automatically jumped to Kate's defense, and she didn't even know her.

"How'd it go with Pruitt?" he asked her. Pruitt had questioned her for nearly an hour.

"I told him everything. You were right. He asked for the notebook, and I handed it over to him. But we've got photocopies and—" she held up her new phone "—photos. I took them when I was waiting to be questioned and texted them to my coworker back in DC. Just in case."

He didn't like what was implied by "just in case." She was right to stay here and not go home. Here, there was a chance he could protect her. It was the least he could do for the sister of the man he let die. His mind swirled into guilt-infused thoughts of that night in the ER, how trauma had slowed his reaction time, just as it did earlier with Craw—

"You okay?"

Logan blinked. "Sorry. What was that?"

"I was asking about Mink. You said he killed a prominent man in town."

"Maybe we should talk about something else."

"Like where we're going. You've been driving in circles for the last five minutes."

"Just making sure we're not followed."

"To where?"

"A safe place for you to stay." He knew that keeping Emma secure was going to be more than he could do alone. He already had a plan; the hard part would be convincing her to go along with it.

A minute later she asked, "The guy Mink killed. What was his name?"

"Jack Murray."

"And this happened ten years ago?"

"Right."

"And was Pruitt the sheriff at that time?"

"No. Just a deputy, I think." He turned onto the next street, staying alert and watching his mirrors.

"Mink and Kate worked for the Murrays back then," he said. "They were both groomers. The Murrays have a stable of high-end Thoroughbreds. Racehorses. Money-makers. Of course, everything the Murrays touch makes money. It's amazing how they were able to adjust and re-coup after the mine was shut down." The bitterness in his voice surprised him. He didn't begrudge the Murrays anything. "That sounded bitter. I'm not. Bitter, I mean. Jack's brother Seth is distant, stays to himself. Probably angry—I don't know. But Lillian, his mother, has been supportive of the clinic. She made a large donation to help get it off the ground."

"Even though Kate was implicated in her son's murder?"

"Kate was never officially implicated. Jack was shot in the stable office. The safe was found open. Cash missing. The police think he was forced at gunpoint to open the safe, then was killed." He stopped and waited for a traffic light to turn green. "Seth was the one who found him."

Emma shuddered. "That's horrible."

"The gun was found in Mink's car the next day, and he was arrested. Kate was never found, and neither was the money. The only evidence against Kate was a necklace spotted near Jack's body, in a pool of blood." He gripped the steering wheel tighter, his palms suddenly sweaty. The description of the murder scene and what Kate must have witnessed that night had haunted him for over ten years. "It was a small cross," he added quietly. "My dad gave it to her. She never took it off."

"That necklace could have been there for any number of reasons."

"That's why the police never brought official charges against Kate, but believe me, she's been tried and condemned in the public eye."

They grew silent as Logan steered along cobblestoned streets, lined with wrought iron luminaires and shaded by the branches of century-old oaks dotting the front yards of immaculately maintained Victorian- and Tudor-style homes. This neighborhood was like a living museum, a snapshot of a historic era built on coal.

On the next street, Logan pointed to a grand two-story redbrick home with white-trimmed bay windows and symmetrical attic dormers. Emma admired the home, then acted surprised when they pulled around the corner and drove down the alley behind the house.

"Where are we?"

"At a friend's house."

"Friends? But I need to find a place to stay and work and—"

"This is it, trust me. You'll be able to rest and work and you'll be safe here, I promise."

"But how can you be sure of that? We don't know who or how—"

"I'm sure because I'm going to be staying here with you. Day and night."

She clamped her mouth shut and stared at him. It was all he could do not to laugh out loud. He'd actually made her blush.

Huey Taylor met them by the back carriage house. He looked to be a fit seventysomething with a strong nose, square jaw and ready smile that went askew as they were introduced. His piercing gray eyes scrutinized her before he winked at Logan and said, "You didn't tell me your friend was a woman. And such a pretty one at that." He held out his arm. "Happy to have you staying in my home, young lady."

She took Huey's arm and let him lead her through a tall iron gate, through an overgrown garden tangled with thistle and bittersweet, and into the back door of the house. Three men sat at the kitchen corner table playing cards. They glanced up and did a double take as Emma approached on Huey's arm. All three stood. The oldest of the three wore a cap with the letters *POW* on the bill. He removed his hat and slightly bowed, a swatch of gray hair falling over his forehead. "Ma'am."

"Gentlemen," Huey said. "This is our new guest, Emma. She'll be staying with us for as long as she needs."

They welcomed her with brief introductions. All military vets, Leo, with the hat, had served in Korea, the other two in Vietnam, both recent widowers. Leo made it clear that, so far, he'd been a lifelong bachelor, but was willing to move into married life if the right woman came along. He said this with a twinkle in his eye. Emma instantly liked him.

Logan passed out the burgers and fries but declined an offer to join the poker game. Instead, he and Emma followed Huey to the fridge, where they grabbed cold sodas, then went through the front room to reach Huey's office, a sunny room with neutral-colored walls dotted with framed black-and-white photos.

They ate their burgers and made small talk, and then a cat appeared and curled around Emma's ankles. A sleek black fellow with a white tuft of fur under his chin and a notched ear.

Huey laughed. "That's Apache. Patch for short, although no one calls him that. Rescued him as a kitten. He's as loyal as they come."

Emma held her soda in one hand and let the other drop to scratch the cat's ears. "Am I picking up on a pattern here? Huey, Apache…"

"Huey flew transport in Vietnam," Logan said. "This is his family home. He's graciously opened it to any veteran who needs a place to stay."

"It's more than that," Huey said. "This is a place for vets who need a family. Against all odds, most of us have outlived our own, so we're like each other's siblings. Fight like them sometimes, too." He laughed a robust belly laugh that thundered through the room. "But all are welcome. Don't matter if you're air force, or navy, or army like your boyfriend here."

Emma's stomach fluttered. Boyfriend? She started to correct his assumption, but the conversation moved on quickly.

"We appreciate the offer to stay," Logan was saying. "I wasn't sure where else we could go." Logan gave him a complete rundown, from Daniel's murder to the most recent attempt on Emma's life outside Crawford's home. "The guy's nervy, breaking into my sister's place, then stalking us and taking shots at Emma in broad daylight, even in a residential area, and we think he's the one who blew up her brother's Jeep and shot at her out in the woods."

Huey looked her over. "What have you got yourself mixed up in, young lady?"

"Whoever this is," Logan said, "he isn't playing games."

Huey agreed. "I'll make sure everyone is alerted to your circumstances. You'll be safe here, Emma." He offered to take them to their rooms. They followed him upstairs and stopped on a landing with two bedrooms and a shared bathroom. Logan would be in the room across from hers.

Huey opened the door to her room, a small dormer with a metal-framed bed tucked neatly under a slanted ceiling. The space was small and cozy, a little like her DC flat, but with cheery yellow walls and a floral-print bedspread instead of her own utilitarian neutrals.

Huey gave a little nod. "I want you to know that it's an honor to serve the family of a law officer. And…and I'm sorry for your loss."

Emma swallowed a lump in her throat. "Thank you. And this is lovely, but I can't stay here long. I can't impose on—"

"If you want to remain in the area to investigate Daniel's

death," Logan said, "then this is the safest place to be. We're in a house full of combat veterans. No one in their right mind would try to break in here."

Emma nodded and thanked Huey for his hospitality, but inside she knew that the person trying to kill her was not in their right mind. He wanted her dead. And the only thing that would keep her safe was finding him before he found her.

The next morning, they enjoyed eggs, bacon and Huey's famous cinnamon rolls, while discussing their plans for the day. Huey insisted that they take his Range Rover. "Whoever's following you is going to be looking for your truck, not a Range Rover. And the windows are tinted, so you won't be as easy to spot."

Logan reluctantly agreed, and they spent the next few hours running errands and picking up personal items for Emma. They also popped by his family home for a few of his things. Rachel and Joe were at work, but Logan was glad to see that Joe had found time to secure the broken kitchen window with plywood.

It was almost one o'clock when they finally arrived at Murray Farms. Logan had spoken with Lillian earlier, arranging to stop by and discuss the upcoming fundraiser for his clinic, but his real motive was to introduce her to Emma, who hoped to get some insight into Daniel's case. If Daniel had pressured Crawford for info on Mink, it likely had to do with Jack Murray's death.

They pulled past the stone gatehouse and meandered down a tree-lined drive toward the expansive brick home with a two-story wraparound porch and black shutters. A continuous white fence lined the way, portioning off rolling pastures dotted with grazing horses. It was all so very picturesque. Logan glanced toward the stable, which was constructed with a white stone foundation, crowned with a cupola, and surrounded by several corrals and other smaller buildings. How often had he seen Kate riding in one of these corrals, caring for the horses? "Kate loved it here. It was like a second home to her."

"How are you doing? This can't be easy."

"It's difficult to visit the memories, but it's also hard to think that I might forget even the tiniest thing about her. It's like a part of me is forever stuck in this strange limbo while the rest of the world keeps on moving forward."

"I know what you mean. I've been feeling that way, too."

He pulled in front of the house and parked next to a walk lined with manicured hedges.

Emma gave him a tentative smile. "Thanks for bringing me here to meet Lillian. Look at this place, though. I've interviewed a lot of people in my career, but I feel a little intimidated here."

"Don't be. You and Lillian will get along great. She's a wonderful person."

He hopped out and opened her door, and a chill overcame him. He pulled the collar up on his new coat and glanced at the stables, where Seth emerged from one of the paddocks leading a striking black horse. Logan waved, but Seth didn't reciprocate. Logan let his hand drop to Emma's elbow and guided her up the walk.

Her own gaze shifted over his shoulder toward the stables. "Is that...?"

"Yes. That's Seth Murray."

The front door popped open, and Lillian Murray stepped onto the porch and embraced him in a hug. "Logan! It's so good to see you." Lillian's long dark hair was streaked with more silver than the last time he'd seen her, but her gaze was as clear, and strong, as ever.

"Lillian," Logan said. "Thank you for taking time for us this morning."

"Taking time for you? You know you're always welcome here." She turned to Emma and took both her hands, giving them a little squeeze. "And how wonderful that you brought someone special with you."

Emma blushed. Logan stumbled for a second, then came around with an introduction. "Emma is a friend. She's visiting the area for a few days."

"I'm so glad you're here. Come on in."

She led them through the foyer and down the hall to a bright room with a small table set with tea, coffee, and trays of cookies and fruit. Lillian poured and chatted briefly about the schedule for the upcoming fundraiser, and a few of the donations that had already been offered for the silent auction, all the while Emma's curious gaze swept the room, taking in the view of the back gardens, a nearby stack of books and a grouping of family photos. Assessing, evaluating and quietly collecting information. Did her mind ever stop working? he wondered.

"Enough business talk," Lillian said, topping off their teacups. "Where are you from, Emma? And what brings you to River Falls?"

"I live in DC now, but I grew up not far from here, outside a town called Siden. You've probably never heard of it."

"I do know of it. That town, like our town, was built on coal."

Emma nodded. "That's right. Built and busted. Siden is practically a ghost town these days."

"River Falls was headed that way when our mine was shut down," Lillian said. "We had to make some difficult decisions and figure out ways to sustain our family and our community. So many people call this little patch of the earth their home, you know."

"Your family saved this town," Logan said.

The corners of Lillian's mouth turned up. "We were fortunate that we had one of the state's largest assets."

Emma leaned forward, with a questioning look on her face.

"Our mountain, of course." Lillian's expression became animated. "White Mountain is one of the highest peaks in the Appalachian range. Not just rich in coal, but also in natural beauty. We saw the possibilities and kick-started most of the ecotourism here, opened the mining museum, and built trails, the lodge and the tram that takes folks to the summit. People come from all over now, for our vistas and especially our beautiful falls. Have you been, Emma?"

"Not since I was a kid. My dad was an outdoorsman, so we came to this area a lot back then."

"And now you live in DC. What do you do there? Are you involved in politics?"

Emma smiled. "No. I could never be a politician. But I do follow politics closely. I'm an investigative journalist."

Lillian seemed delighted. "You are? Who do you work for?"

"Whoever pays me." Emma laughed. "I work for the National Division of Investigative Journalists. We research and write stories for all the major news outlets across the nation. It's not as intriguing as it sounds." She shrugged and looked Logan's way. "But like Logan, I feel called to that type of work."

The reminder that Emma had another life back in DC made Logan uncomfortable for some reason. He was more than happy to redirect the conversation. "We really appre-

ciate you taking time to see us this morning," he said to
Lillian.

"It's so wonderful to have you two here, but there must
be something on your mind, Logan. Is it the clinic?"

"No. Everything is fine at the clinic. Something else has
come up." He hesitated. "I almost hate to mention it because
I don't want to upset you."

"Oh?"

"It has to do with Jack's murder."

Lillian's expression soured. "Yes. That's always a difficult discussion."

"I'm sorry, but Emma just recently lost her brother and—"

Lillian's hand jutted out over the table and connected
with Emma's. "Oh, no. Your brother? I'm so sorry, dear."

Logan noticed Emma's shoulders curve inward. "Yes,"
she said. "He was killed just a few weeks back. Daniel
Hayes."

Lillian's eyes searched the air. "Daniel Hayes…?"

Logan filled in the blanks. "He was a deputy sheriff
killed in the line of duty."

Lillian nodded. "Yes, I remember now. I'm so sorry,
Emma."

"The thing is," Logan continued, "right before he died,
Daniel had reopened Jack's case."

"He did? Why wasn't I aware of this?"

"He didn't come out to talk to you or interview you?"
Emma asked.

"No. But maybe he tried and couldn't reach me. I was
out of town for a while, and… I believe I was gone at the
time your brother was killed. I heard about it after I came
back home. Did they find the person who killed him?"

"No, I'm afraid not."

"Such a tragedy."

Logan noticed a slight tremor in the woman's fingers. This whole topic was more difficult to discuss than he'd imagined it would be. He felt bad for upsetting Lillian, but their need for answers kept him pushing forward. "Is it possible that Daniel had interviewed Seth?"

"I'm sure he would have told me, if that were the case." She bit out the words and pinned Emma with a stare. "Why was your brother looking into my son's murder? All that was resolved years ago. The man who killed him is in prison, where he belongs."

Emma's gaze darted his way, then back to Lillian. "We think new evidence came to light."

"Evidence? That's silly. There was a very thorough investigation at the time. Without a doubt Michael Kincaid was guilty. The jury didn't even deliberate their verdict. The whole thing is over."

"Not all of it," Logan interjected.

Lillian stared at him, her features crumbling. "Of course. Kate. I know that haunts your family, and I'm so sorry, you know I am, but..." She touched her fingertips to her temple. "You were right. This is all very upsetting. I don't want to discuss it anymore."

Logan softened his tone. "If you could just answer a couple more questions. It's important. There may be a chance that my family can finally get some answers about Kate."

Lillian shook her head. "I understand. I do. Maybe later. I'm not feeling well." She stood. "If you'll excuse me, I'm afraid we're going to have to cut our visit—"

She collapsed forward over the table. A teacup fell and shattered.

Emma gasped, "Oh, no!"

Logan jumped into action, scooping Lillian off the table, carrying her away from the sharp fragments of the broken cup and lowering her gently to the floor. She was pale and covered in a thin sheen of sweat. He fumbled to check her pulse, his fingers trembling over the surface of her skin, unable to focus on her heart rate. *What is wrong with me?*

"Go out to the barn and find Seth," he told Emma. "Tell him to hurry. I'll call 911."

Emma ran to the barn, her lungs burning as she reached the entrance. She burst inside and shouted, "Seth!" She blinked, her eyes trying to cope against the darkness. She could make out several rough wooden stalls, a tack room lined with bridles and leads, saddles, metal water buckets and feed barrels. It smelled of sour urine, sweet hay, polished leather. A horse snorted at her from one of the stalls.

"Seth?" she yelled again, rushing toward the back of the barn and around a stack of hay bales. She stopped and listened—rustling hay, hooves stamping, a drawn-out horse whinny, boards creaking and now sirens in the distance—but no sign of Seth. *He was just here. Where did he go?* She headed back the way she'd come, then heard two men's voices, as if far away, saying something about banks. She was about to call out when she saw a closed door adjacent to the tack room. The barn's office? Maybe Seth was in there.

She knocked and pushed the door open on squeaky hinges, her gaze drawn to a massive safe behind a marred oak desk. Her mind painted a picture of it hanging open, while Jack Murray lay on the floor, blood oozing from his bullet-ravaged body. She squeezed her eyes shut against the unbidden image, and the floorboard creaked behind her. She wheeled and found herself standing face-to-face with Seth Murray, his chin tilted as if defying any interference. His icy stare made her back up, every fiber of her body on high alert.

"Seth Murray?"

"Who are you?"

Out of the corner of her eye, she saw a tall, thin man leaving through one of the back paddocks. He skirted off to the side as if sneaking away and climbed into a dark SUV. A cold chill scrabbled up her spine. *The man from the woods?*

She met Seth's gaze full-on. "It's your mother," she said. "She's collapsed."

SIX

Logan slouched on a plastic chair next to Emma in the waiting room, his elbows on his knees and his head buried in his hands, staring at the floor, trying to make sense of things. Seth sat on the other side of the waiting room. Logan had tried to talk to him a couple of times, but he'd asked to be left alone. Understandable. During his time as a doctor, Logan had learned that everyone handled stress differently. Which was why he shouldn't have pushed Lillian so far. He'd upset her, maybe enough to cause her collapse. And then he couldn't take care of her.

He thought his flashbacks would go away on their own, or that maybe more rest would fix things, but it was apparent that he needed extra help. Even now, just being back in the ER for the first time since Daniel's death caused him to feel anxious. Thankfully, another doctor was on staff today. A capable doctor.

The desk nurse called Seth's name. They spoke for a second, and then she showed him through the double doors leading to the ER. Logan watched him go, then lowered his gaze to the floor again.

He felt Emma's hand on his back, reassuring him, supporting him. "This isn't your fault, Logan," she whispered.

He straightened. "I knew my questions would upset her. I still pushed her."

"The questions needed to be asked."

He shook his head. "Maybe, but still, I've known Lillian for a long time. She was a friend of my mother. Almost like an aunt to me."

Emma's fingers tensed on his back. He straightened and turned her way. "What is it?"

"Nothing."

He didn't believe that. Over the past few days, he'd come to know Emma well enough to read her emotions. "You didn't like Lillian, did you?"

"No, it's not that. I liked her. She was gracious and welcoming and everything. It's just that I interview a lot of people for my work, and I've become good at reading when people are hiding things. Lillian knows more than she was telling us."

Logan trusted Emma's instincts, but he knew it could be easy to misread people, especially when the topic was highly emotional.

Emma leaned closer. "When I went to find Seth out in the barn, he was with a thin man, like the guy who shot at me in the woods."

"There are a lot of thin guys out there. It could have just been a groomer or stable hand. They have a half dozen people working those stables."

"The guy didn't want to be seen. He snuck out the back paddock. And Seth gives me a bad feeling."

"Why?"

"Instinct, I guess."

Logan didn't know what to say to that, so he sat back and slipped into his own thoughts. They waited for another half hour. The emergency room doors opened and closed several times, and people came and went. A red-faced, screaming toddler and a frazzled-looking mother took up residence across the room. Logan knew he should be patient, but the crying was making him more frustrated. Just when he thought he couldn't take another second of the kid's screaming, Seth came out, his face red and angry as he marched their way.

Logan stood. "Seth. How is she?"

"She's fine, no thanks to you. Apparently, you were asking her questions about Jack's murder. Why? You upset her with your questions."

"That wasn't my intent. We were just—"

"I don't want to hear it. And I don't care if you're friends with my mother or not, just stay away from her. She's fragile. I won't have you upsetting her again." His face was awash with anger. "Your family is nothing but trouble. Always has been."

Logan locked stares with Seth, anticipating a derogatory comment about Kate. Snippets of past accusations, whispered behind his back by townsfolk, assaulted his memory: *She's a murderer, a thief. She took the money and ran.* Logan gritted his teeth and pushed past his emotions. Alienating Seth wouldn't get them the answers they needed for Emma. Still, every muscle in his body tensed and coiled like a snake about to strike.

Emma's hand connected with his. "We're so very sorry about Lillian," he heard her say, as she gently tugged him away. "Come on. We should go."

She pulled him through the door, dropping his hand once they were outside. He inhaled the cold air, clearing the haze of emotion that had enveloped him. "Thanks. I was starting to lose my perspective in there."

"I could tell."

Obviously, nothing had really changed, Logan thought. Seth still thought Kate was a murderer. And he still harbored anger and didn't feel forgiving toward Seth. His reaction had surprised him. He'd thought he'd worked through all those old feelings of betrayal and hurt, but apparently not. Logan grimaced and balled his fist, then checked himself, but not before Emma noticed.

"What is it?" she asked. "There's something more between you and Seth than what you've told me, isn't there?"

"Yeah, but I thought I'd worked through it all." Hadn't God heard his prayers asking for help in forgiving? Why did the anger still churn so close to the surface? He let out a long sigh. "Back then, when news of Jack's murder broke out, Seth was one of the first to insist that Kate was involved in the killing. He's a big man in town, and his word carried weight with the locals. He painted Kate in a bad light, said that she was motivated by greed, being that she was dirt-poor and from a mining family."

They came to his truck, and he unlocked her door, holding it open until she got situated in the seat. He climbed behind the wheel and started the engine, adjusting the heater.

"It couldn't have been easy to hear that about your sister and your family," Emma said. "I'm sorry. People can be so cruel."

"It wasn't easy. But what bothers me the most is my own reaction back there with Seth." He turned and faced her. Opening up like this was a challenge for him. He never was one to talk about his faith. "Back then, I was young. Kate was gone and my family was devastated. As rumors started and people began to talk, especially Seth, I became bitter. It took someone special to set me straight."

"Huey?"

"Yeah. After Dad died, Huey became a mentor to me.

He saw that my grief over Kate was destroying me. All that bitterness was turning me into someone I didn't want to be, so I needed to make some changes to move forward."

"What type of changes?"

"Huey helped me see that sometimes when we don't have answers for the things that happen to us in life, it's easy to make up our own stories and our own villains. Seth blamed Kate, which wasn't hard to do with her not around to defend herself. And I got angry at everyone. Mostly Seth. He was on the news a lot, speaking poorly of my sister and her boyfriend. Huey helped me see how pain and grief can distort our view. He helped me turn that anger over to God and trust in His mercy and justice."

"I admire that you were able to do that."

Logan laughed. "No, that's the thing. Just now, back there with Seth, all that anger came rushing back. I thought I'd worked through it a long time ago, but I felt like I was going to tear the guy apart."

"I saw that."

"Did I scare you?"

"No. I was surprised, but not afraid."

"Good. Because I scared myself."

They sat in silence, each lost in their thoughts. He wondered what Emma was thinking. He couldn't read her. *Why did I tell her so much? What does she think of me now? And what will she think once she knows Daniel died under my care?*

It was late afternoon and the sun was behind the clouds, and even in the truck he could feel the sudden drop in the temperature. He zipped his coat higher, cranked up the heater and realized that he hadn't eaten since the tea and cookies at Lillian's house. "I'm starved. How about you?"

"Yeah. Definitely."

"There's a place not far from here that has great pizza. Let's see if Rachel and Joe can meet us."

Joe was working late, but Rachel was able to join them, and ten minutes later, the three of them sat in a cozy booth by the front window, a pitcher of soda between them. Emma took in her surroundings. The pizzeria was welcoming, with rough wood floors and ceiling beams that fit perfectly with the well-worn red-and-white-plaid oilcloth table coverings. The warmth from the stone oven and aromas of yeast crusts and cheeses baking didn't hurt, either.

After the waitress took their order, Logan told Rachel about their visit to Murray Farms and how Lillian had ended up in the hospital. "It was horrible," Emma added. "Her collapsing all of a sudden like that."

"I bet," Rachel said. "What do you think caused it?"

Emma glanced at Logan, then said, "Hard to know. Seth was there at the hospital, but we didn't talk much."

Soda splashed on the table as Logan refilled his glass from the pitcher. He snatched a napkin and sopped it up.

Rachel lifted her chin and eyed her brother. "Well, I do have some news about Jake Crawford. It's not good, I'm afraid. After you told me about what happened, I called a nurse friend of mine who works at the hospital. She said he's in bad shape. And there's been a police officer positioned outside his room the whole time. Just thought you might want to know."

Logan wadded the wet napkin and slid it behind the cheese and pepper flake holder. "Pruitt must think he's still under threat. Interesting." He went on to tell her what Crawford had said right before he was shot, and how he thought it might be related to Jack Murray's murder. "He mentioned Mink."

"Mink?" Rachel flinched. She took a quick breath and forced a smile Emma's way. "Sorry. Mink was Kate's boyfriend. It's still so difficult after all these years."

"Don't be sorry," Emma said, reaching across the table to touch her arm. "I understand."

Rachel pulled back and dabbed at her eyes with a napkin. "So, you're thinking that Daniel was investigating Jack Murray's case, and Crawford was shot because he knew something?"

Emma nodded. "It looks like it. Do you remember much about that night Jack Murray was murdered?"

"I was twenty at the time." Rachel sat back in the booth and sighed. "Kate was almost four years younger than me. I remember it was late and she wasn't home yet. Which was weird. She never came home late. We called everyone we knew, but no one had seen her. Mom paced the floor waiting for her to turn into the driveway."

"She didn't," Logan said. "But the cops did. That's when we found out that Murray was dead. Deputies had come by the house looking for Kate."

Silence settled between them as they both mentally replayed the events of that night.

Emma spoke up. "Do either of you remember anything strange about Kate's behavior leading up to that night?"

Logan shook his head. "No, not really."

"I do." Rachel absently smoothed her napkin over the table. "Kate had been upset because one of her favorite mares had lost her foal the day before. She was sad for the mother mare. She'd been spending extra time at the stable, trying to comfort her. Sounds silly, but it was so like Kate. She spent hours with the horses. They became like friends to her."

"I remember that," Logan said. "But what would the mare losing her foal have to do with anything?"

"Nothing, just that... I don't know, Logan. I've tried so hard to put that day out of my memory, but I remember Kate being upset that morning before going to work at the stables. I overheard her on the phone. She was arguing with Mink, and I think it had something to do with that mare."

They stopped talking as the waitress appeared and placed a steaming pan of pizza in the middle of the table. Emma took a couple of slices, sprinkled on cheese and said, "I'd like to visit Mink at the prison."

"I don't think that's a good idea," Rachel said.

Logan's stomach clenched. Mink, and a prison full of men gawking at her. He didn't like the way that sounded. "No way."

Emma shot him a look. "Crawford mentioned him in connection to Daniel's questions. He may have key information."

Logan shook his head. "I don't like the idea of you in a male prison."

"This is the type of stuff I do all the time for my work. I've interviewed prisoners before. I interviewed several of Victor Duran's gang members."

Logan's jaw twitched. "You shouldn't go out there alone."

"She shouldn't be going out there at all," Rachel protested.

Emma picked up one of her pizza slices and locked her gaze on Logan. "We can drive over together," she said, taking a small bite. "But I'll want to talk to him alone. He'd open up more if it's just me."

"You'll go with or without me, won't you?"

"I'm determined to get my answers."

Rachel shook her head. "No, no, no. What are you two doing?" Her voice hitched as she continued. "Emma, you've been shot at twice now. Your car blown up. Obviously, someone is serious about keeping a secret. Serious enough that they killed your brother when he got too close to the truth. I think you ought to leave all of this up to the sheriff."

"We've already told Pruitt everything," Logan assured her.

"Yeah," Emma added. "And he's not dedicating anyone to our personal protection."

Logan agreed. "Emma and I are under threat, and there's no time to wait around for the sheriff's department to figure things out." Not to mention that they suspected someone in the sheriff's department might be involved.

"Logan is right," Emma said. "We can't wait—"

"Yes, you can wait," Rachel bit out. "Logan is a doctor, not an investigative journalist like you."

"Rachel?" Logan was surprised by his sister's reaction.

"It's true," Rachel countered. "Most people would leave this up to the police, not dive in and investigate on their own, taking risks and getting shot at."

"I've been shot at before," Logan reminded her. "When I served our country."

"And you're still suffering from it."

Logan felt Emma's stare. His face burned hot with embarrassment.

"Please don't do this," Rachel pleaded with him. "Leave it all alone and in the past, where it belongs."

Logan reached across the table and took his sister's hands in his. "This may be a chance to find out what happened to Kate."

"I know that. That's not it... I just..." Tears streamed down Rachel's face. "We've talked about this before. We know Kate can't be alive. She would never have left us, especially not Mom. She'd never do that to Mom."

"Then what are you afraid of?"

"Kate, then Mom and Dad… They're all gone. You're all that I have and…and I'm pregnant."

Emma smiled. "Congratulations, Rachel. That's great news."

The tension around the table instantly eased.

"I'm going to be an uncle?" Logan asked. "An uncle?" He squeezed Rachel's hands. "I can't believe it. I'm going to be an uncle."

She pulled back, her eyes blazing. "Listen to me. This baby will never know its aunt Kate or its grandparents, but I want it to know its uncle. So, you need to stop looking into all of this and quit putting yourself in danger. Leave it to the authorities."

"I get it, sis. I do. But for years I've been asking God to help me find Kate, or at least know what happened to her, and now He's given me that opportunity. I can't turn my back on that." He reached out again. "Try to understand—"

"No. Don't do this." She batted his hands away. "And don't talk to me about God. God has not been here for me or our family for a long time." Her hands flew to her mouth. "I'm sorry. I don't really believe that. I don't. It's just that there's been so much, and things were starting to seem normal again."

The pizza soured in Emma's stomach. The last thing she wanted to do was hurt Rachel. She'd had so much pain in her life, and this baby was supposed to be a time of joy.

Logan leaned forward. "Even if this had nothing to do with Kate, you can't expect me to turn my back on Emma. Someone is trying to kill her."

"No," Emma said. "Rachel's right. You hardly know me, and this is too dangerous. I can take things from here."

Logan insisted, "Absolutely not. Listen, both of you. I

spent four years risking my life to protect freedom and defending people I'll never meet my whole life, but I know you, Emma, and respect you, and if either of you think I'm going to let someone—"

"Okay, okay." Rachel swiped at her wet cheeks with the napkin. "You're right. And I wouldn't expect anything less from you. Only I'm afraid of…" Her voice faded. "I want to help you, too, Emma. It's just that I'm an emotional mess. I'm sorry."

"No need to apologize," Emma said. "I understand."

Rachel smiled through her tears. "Thank you." She let out a long sigh, blew her nose and changed the topic. "Where are you two staying?"

Logan cleared his throat and shot Emma a look as he jumped in to answer, "With friends. Somewhere safe." He hadn't had time to warn her about not telling anyone their location, not even Rachel.

"You can't tell me?"

"I don't want to put you and Joe and—" he glanced at her belly "—and the baby in danger. I'm not sure what we're dealing with here. We'll be safe where we're at."

Rachel straightened. "I'll keep things going the best I can at the clinic. You planned to be away at the cabin this week anyway, so there's nothing pressing." She rubbed at her temples. "I'm so worried. That's all."

"I'll keep us safe," Logan promised.

Emma stared at the table. *Safe.* She hadn't felt safe since Daniel died. He'd been a good man, a good cop, but God took him. And the last few days she'd been skirting death just to learn the truth. But hearing Logan's promise now, a calm swept through her body and warmed her heart.

Rachel's phone rang, interrupting the moment. She looked at the display, her face lighting up. "It's Joe," she said and

answered. Emma took another bite of pizza and averted her
eyes from Logan. Outside, a gray sports car pulled up to the
curb. Was this the same car that was parked across the street
from Rachel and Joe's place? Emma leaned forward and
squinted through the glass, dread pooling in the pit of her
stomach. She stared in horror as the window rolled down,
revealing a man with an assault rifle.

SEVEN

"Get down!" Emma shouted. She grabbed for Rachel, and they dived to the ground, Logan hovering over them using his own body as a shield. Above them, glass shattered as a spray of bullets peppered the walls, the ceiling and the high wood backs of the booths. Over the sound of bullets, Emma heard a woman scream and a baby cry, voices shouting and an outbreak of soft sobs. Rachel's sobs, and finally silence.

Dust and a sharp burnt smell clouded the air, and more high-pitched ringing filled Emma's head. Logan stood and surveyed the scene, before helping them from the floor. The car was gone. Emma took Rachel's icy hands in hers and stared at her belly. "Are you okay? Is the baby okay?"

"I think so."

The cook and waitress rushed toward them, and then bystanders on the street flooded the restaurant. Everyone spoke at once. *Did you see the shooter? Anyone call the cops? Do you need an ambulance?* A soft mewing sound escaped Rachel's lips as she swayed back and forth. Emma wrapped her arms around her and pulled her close, but it was an effort to stand and hold her when Emma's own body felt like it wanted to give up. She steadied herself, swallowed back a lump in her throat and looked to Logan for help.

He gently placed his hand on the small of her back. "You're doing great, Emma. Let's move to the back, away from all this," he said, guiding them away from the group. He got Rachel settled in a booth and made a phone call, then pulled Emma aside. "The police should be here any second. I called Joe. He's on his way to get Rachel."

"Good." Emma wondered if Logan regretted his earlier words about sticking with her through all this. No doubt she was the intended target. And now Rachel had almost been caught in the cross fire. "I'm sorry, I'm sorry," Emma said, over and over. But her apology seemed inadequate, and her words felt forced.

Logan frowned. "This isn't your fault. You're just trying to do what's right. Whoever's behind all this is the bad guy, not you, Emma. And feeling guilty won't help." His hand rested gently on hers. "After you shouted, all I saw was the rifle. Nothing else. Did you get a look at the driver? Was it the same guy that shot at you in the woods?"

"I don't know. All I saw was dark hair. And the gun. But I saw the car the other day at Rachel and Joe's, parked by the curb. I assumed it belonged to one of their neighbors."

"It was gray, wasn't it?"

"Yeah, a sports car. It looked expensive." She glanced at Rachel, pale and folded in on herself. *How long will it take Joe to get here?*

Logan ran his fingers through his hair until it spiked out in dark tufts. "Whoever did this feels threatened by whatever was in that notebook. They were shooting to kill and didn't care if there was collateral damage."

Emma's stomach reeled. Reality was catching up to her. They'd almost died. Rachel almost died. And her baby. "But there's nothing in that notebook." Did they think there was more? And then she realized that whoever did this thought she still had the notebook, and since she'd given it to Pruitt, this shooting crossed him off the list of suspects. Or were they after something else? Did she miss something at the cabin? Something they assumed she had found?

Several deputies showed up and took control of the scene. Joe also arrived and went straight to Rachel. He spoke to her calmly, and she nodded, swiping under her eyes. Black streaked across her cheeks as the EMTs began checking her over.

A deputy took their statements, and then Pruitt arrived and singled Emma out for questioning. Mostly the same questions they'd already asked each other. *What type of car? Did you see the driver? Which direction did he come from? Can you describe the weapon?* On and on, and then a question Emma didn't expect: "Did you remove anything from the notebook before turning it over to us?"

"No. Nothing." Were pages missing from the notebook? She hadn't noticed.

Pruitt's stare unnerved her. "Did you find anything else at that cabin?" he asked.

She shook her head.

"Ms. Hayes, you're a reporter—"

"Journalist. I investigate stories. Reporters report the story. A lot of journalists work as reporters, but not all reporters are journalists."

"Journalist, reporter, whatever. Are you holding something back for the sake of a good story?"

"For a *story*?" Emma's blood boiled. "These people are my friends. And the story is my own brother's death. And my audience, Sheriff, if you really want to know, is my mother and father, who are grieving the death of their only son. So please don't accuse me of playing games with evidence. I'm not looking for a *story*, but the *truth*, Sheriff."

Pruitt's eyes blazed at the word *truth*. He took a breath, then offered, "I'm sorry you lost your brother. He was one of us, one of my men. I'm sick about his death. But he was killed in the line of duty while making a traffic stop."

"Was he wearing a body cam? I'd like to see—"

"Body cams are still optional in West Virginia. And I'm afraid our department's budget is limited. Look, Ms. Hayes. Don't you think that if I thought he was murdered by someone other than the guy he pulled over, I'd be all over it?"

"If that's true, then why is someone so intent on killing me?"

"Maybe you ticked off the wrong person with your reporting."

She'd angered a lot of people in her short career. It was the nature of the game. "Have you compared the bullets yet, Sheriff?"

"What are you talking about?"

"The bullet that shot Crawford and the bullet that killed my brother. Are they the same caliber? From the same gun? Crawford's name was in Daniel's notebook, so there's a reason to believe that he was shot because he knew something."

"Unless *you* were the target? And Crawford was just at the wrong place at the wrong time. I read up on you. I commend your work. What you did was admirable. You helped put a major drug lord in prison, and that took some guts, but that type of reporting makes a lot of enemies. Dangerous enemies."

Emma wasn't going to be distracted by his flattery. "You could be right, especially if the caliber of the bullet that shot Crawford is unrelated to these cases. But if the bullets are a match, then it confirms a connection. Whether that connection is between Daniel and Crawford or between Daniel and me searching his cabin. Either way, it would be clear Daniel was killed by someone with something more in mind than random traffic rage."

The vein in Pruitt's temple throbbed angrily. "I know how to do my job, Ms. Hayes."

She took a step forward, her eyes locked on the man. "Do you?"

Logan gently tugged her arm, bringing her back to reality. She shrank, her cheeks burning with shame. That last comment was unnecessary, mean even. And now she'd alienated the one person who could help her get information. What was wrong with her? She knew better. Still, she shook off Logan's hand and pushed further. "I have your coroner's report for Daniel, and it lists the bullet as being a .380 caliber. Was that the same caliber used to shoot Mr. Crawford?"

"I'm sorry," Pruitt said. "I can't really discuss the details of Crawford's case with you."

"I feel like I have the right to know, Sheriff. My brother is dead, and someone is trying to kill me. Did the bullets match or not? Tell me."

Pruitt ignored her and stepped away to speak to Deputy Davis. Emma hadn't noticed her there. Had she heard her whole outburst? It was bad enough that Logan, still standing behind her, had heard the bitterness in her.

Pruitt and Davis spoke in whispers, making it impossible for Emma to figure out what they were saying. Finally, they finished, and Pruitt took off through the restaurant to talk to the scene techs. Deputy Davis came over, her demeanor subdued. "I'm sorry your families are going through so much." She looked between Emma and Logan.

Emma stood motionless. Her eyes stung with frustration and guilt over what she was putting the Greer family through. "I'm just trying to find out what type of gun was used to shoot Crawford. I think there might be a connection to—"

"I can't discuss the case with you, but I can tell you that Danny talked about his family, and you, all the time. He loved you all. He wouldn't want you to be in this type of danger."

Daniel talked to her about family? Emma wondered if her brother and Deputy Davis had more than coworkers. He hadn't mentioned a woman in his life. "I hadn't met many of his friends here in River Falls. I'm sorry for that. We were both caught up in our work lately and..."

"That's understandable. Life is so busy these days. We're all just doing the best we can."

Emma stared at the floor, trying to rein in her emotions.

Davis continued, "Being a cop is more than a full-time job, and Danny was one of the best on the force. No one could ever live up to his dedication. Or daring ways." She sighed. "I could tell you stories about him that you wouldn't believe."

Emma glanced up. "I'd love to hear them," she said. Deputy Davis's features had softened. Emma thought she was very pretty after all.

"We should get together, maybe coffee or something, and exchange a few stories. It'd be good for both of us."

Emma felt herself brighten. "I'd like that."

"Good. I need to get back to work now," the deputy said. "But here's my card. Text me your number and we'll make plans."

"Are you okay?" Logan asked as soon as the deputy was out of earshot.

"Everything is catching up to me, that's all." Emma crossed her arms over her chest and looked at Rachel and Joe as they huddled together in the booth. "And now your family is being hurt, and all because of—"

"No. Don't go there. We're going to get through this."
His voice, calm and firm, washed over her.

She wanted to nod to acknowledge his reassurance, but
despite trying to hold it together, tears started flowing.
Everything she'd done was only making things worse. She
tried to turn away, but Logan reached out and pulled her to
him, wrapping his arms around her. She leaned into him
and let the tears fall.

Pruitt kept everyone at the scene for another hour for more
questioning. Joe had to stay in town to work but planned to
take Rachel down to his parents' house in Hinton, where she
could rest. Logan agreed and was relieved to know Rachel
and the baby would be somewhere safe. Now he turned all
his focus to Emma. There was a strength about Emma, but
vulnerability, too. And more than anything, he wanted to
protect her. Listening to her talk to Pruitt, Logan realized
that he could no longer hide the fact that he was the doctor
the night Daniel came into the ER. He had information that
her life depended on. His life, too.

As soon as they were back on the road, he pulled over in
a strip mall parking lot, cut the engine and turned to Emma,
his palms sweating as he searched for the right words to
tell her about Daniel. People passed by as they walked to
and from their parked cars. He wished they were someplace else but was glad for the tinted windows in Huey's
Range Rover. At least they had some privacy. He had no
idea how she would react. Her attitude toward him had softened since she broke down at the restaurant. Since he'd held
her. If he was honest, something in him had shifted, too.
She'd felt good in his arms. Really good, and he realized
that he'd longed to hold her ever since he found her in the
woods. But what would happen once she knew the truth?

He wouldn't blame her if she hated him for what he'd done. Or rather, hadn't done.

She was staring at him. "Why are we stopped here? What's up?"

"There's something I need to tell you, and I don't think it should wait."

His mind raced in a dozen different directions. How should he start?

"Does this have something to do with the way I questioned Pruitt about the bullets? I was aggressive, I know. That was the journalist in me coming out."

"Yeah, it has to do with that, but not how you think. When you mentioned the autopsy report, you said that the bullet was a .380. Are you sure about that?"

"Yes. I'm sure."

"The bullet that came out of Daniel was not a .380. It was a 9 mm. I know because—"

"But the autopsy said it was a .380."

"That might have been what it said, but... Thing is, if the autopsy report said .380, then someone altered it. It could have been Pruitt, or someone else in the chain of command, or—"

"I don't get it. What makes you think it was altered? How would you know?"

"I was an army medic, remember? I pulled bullets out of soldiers all the time and—"

"But how would you— Wait—*you* pulled the bullet out of Daniel? You operated on him?" Her voice shook, her eyes round with questions.

"I'm sorry. I wanted to tell you earlier. I just didn't know how." He tried to read her expression. Was it sadness or anger? "I don't want there to be any secrets between us. I—"

"Was he in pain? Please tell me that he wasn't in pain." Her voice choked on the last word.

Of course that was what she would be worried about. How insensitive of him to just spring it on her like this. Her eyes met his with an intensity that he'd not seen before. He warred within himself, flooded with both guilt for causing her sadness and an instinctive desire to hold her, to ease her sorrow. "No pain. He was unconscious when he arrived in the ER. And the paramedics had already administered those meds."

"Did he...did he wake up at all? Did he say anything?" Her voice broke and her expression faltered.

This was too much for her. Why hadn't he anticipated this? "No. Nothing. I'm sorry."

Tears streamed over her cheeks as she leaned across the center console and pressed her head into his shoulder. He turned in his seat and held her face, tracing his thumb over a tear wet on her skin. "I'm so sorry," he whispered, over and over. "I'm so sorry."

"Don't be sorry. It's okay," she assured him. "I know you did everything you could for him."

Her confidence in him twisted his gut; her brother had died while he'd sat paralyzed, prisoner to his painful past. He was about to tell her the rest of the story when she pulled back and wiped her face. "It brings me so much comfort to know you were the doctor on charge that night. I can't think of anyone better to be with Daniel in the end."

He bit back his words, and a dull ache settled in his heart.

EIGHT

The next morning, a screeching sound outside pulled Emma from the fog of sleep. She fumbled for her phone on the nightstand and blinked at the screen, fighting for full alertness. Six o'clock already. In less than an hour, Deputy Davis would be waiting for her at the coffee shop.

She withdrew from the warmth of her covers and crossed the room to the window, parting the heavy drapes. Sunlight stung her eyes. Her room and the room across the hall where Logan slept were converted from the home's attic and overlooked Huey's quaint, historic neighborhood, with Victorian-style streetlamps and cobblestoned roads, and colorful rooflines that peeked through the treetops.

She forced the windowpane up and leaned out, breathing in the fresh air. Several large, screeching black birds lined a bare branch outside her window. A breeze shook the treetops, they took flight, and bright leaves tumbled down to an orange-and-gold forest carpet over the backyard. From somewhere in the house, she heard voices, laughter and the clinking of dishes, and her gaze turned to the mountains, which glowed in the horizon beyond River Falls. She was overcome with awe at the beauty of God's creation, but then a darkness settled over her, as she recalled a verse from

Scripture about moving mountains with faith as small as a mustard seed.

She turned away, knowing that her faith these days couldn't move a single speck of dirt.

She hit the shower, and as she dressed, her mind turned over the most recent events, especially the gun caliber. Had someone doctored the autopsy? And Pruitt's hard-lined questions about whether she'd found something else at the cabin had surprised her. She hadn't had time to do anything other than retrieve the notebook and run. Had she missed something? She wanted to search the cabin again, maybe find a spent cartridge, so she at least had a sample of the caliber fired at her from the woods. Maybe Pruitt was right. That one of Duran's men was chasing her out there. The thought disturbed her, but she shook it off and focused on her day. First coffee with Deputy Davis, and then an interview at the prison with Mink.

A little while later, Emma walked into the café and in-haled the aroma of fresh ground coffee, sweet warm cara-mel and a tinge of cinnamon and wondered if there was anything better than the smell of a coffee shop. She scanned the room and easily spotted Deputy Davis in her uniform. She was holding a spot in line.

Emma caught up to her. "Deputy Davis, thanks for meet-ing with me. Sorry if I'm late."

"No. Not at all. And call me Jess. But not when Pruitt is around." She smiled. "This is going to take a while. The place is always packed like this, especially on Fridays. Afraid I come here every morning before my shift. Can't go a single day without my sugar and caffeine. They're my main source of fuel for the day."

She and the deputy finally worked their way through the line, picked up their coffees at the counter and settled at a round table in the back of the small café. "Danny would meet me here a lot of mornings. Sometimes we'd go out after shift, too, you know, just to compare days. Even after the worst day, he could make me laugh. Your brother had the most wicked sense of humor. But I don't have to tell you that."

"No. That's one of the things I miss most about him," Emma confided. "And his laugh. I was always the more serious one, but Daniel knew how to have fun."

"Yes, he did. We became instant friends. Which is kind of rare, especially in this line of work. It's not often I meet someone who I feel a connection with. Someone I can trust like I trusted Danny."

"I know what you mean," Emma said, thinking of Logan. As a journalist, she tended to be cautious warming up to others. But what had it been? A little less than a week and already she felt like she'd known Logan forever. She considered him a true friend. Even this morning, he'd gone out of his way to drive her to the coffee shop and then insisted on waiting in the lot for her. He was protecting her, and Emma found it endearing. Warmth rushed through her as she remembered how she felt safe and cherished in his arms. Knowing his hands were the ones to tend to Daniel in his dying moments brought Logan even closer to her. Maybe it was just a coincidence, but it felt like a small miracle to her that the man who had saved her life and now stood by her as she sought the truth was also the man who was there when Daniel took his last breath. She shook her head and took a sip of coffee to refocus.

"Were you and Daniel partners?" she asked.

"We went out on some calls together. It's a small department and usually we don't pair up for patrol. But…" Jess cleared her throat.

A crack in the deputy's tough exterior. Emma's heart poured out to the woman. She was so caught up in her own family's loss that she didn't think too much about Daniel's friends and coworkers. He'd been here for almost two years. It made sense that he would have developed some meaningful relationships.

"I'm sorry. It sounds like you and Daniel were close."

"We were close friends," Jess said. She took a sip of her latte and nodded her head. "To be honest, sometimes I wished it was more. But he never asked me out."

"Oh. Was he dating someone else? He never talked about anyone, but—"

"I don't think so. I'm not sure when he would have met anyone. He was single-minded, you know. Work, work, work. That's about it. I tried, but...well..."

Emma didn't know what to say to that, so she switched topics. "Did you two go to the same church?"

Jess's eyes grew wide. "Church? Uh...no. If we hung out after work, it was just to grab a burger or something. Faith never came up. I don't think I ever heard him mention church."

Emma felt like she'd just been stabbed in the heart. Daniel was always the more faithful one. She'd always looked up to him as an example. Had he drifted from his faith?

Jess took another long sip of her coffee. "Mostly we talked about current cases, department politics, that type of stuff. But he did talk about your parents. He told me about their anniversary party last year and how much they loved the quilt."

"Aw...yes, the quilt." She and Daniel had spent hours poring over old photographs to make a memory quilt for their parents' thirty-fifth wedding anniversary. They'd loved it. It'd become her mother's favorite gift, always proudly displayed in the family room, where she'd bore the neighbors to death, showing them each picture. The night they'd learned about Daniel's death, Dad said that her mother buried herself in the quilt, weeping. Tears pricked the edges of Emma's eyes.

"I didn't mean to upset you," Jess said.

Emma forced a smile. "No. You didn't. Memories are bittersweet, that's all."

Jess drew in a deep breath and started to say something, then stopped.

"What is it?" Emma asked.

"I was at Danny's service. You probably don't remember. There were so many people there."

"No. I think I do remember seeing you."

"Really? Well…anyway, I had this with me, and I was going to give it to your mom, but things were so hectic, and, well, I planned to mail it to her at some point, but, uh, I think you should have it." She reached down where she'd set a duffel bag on the floor by her chair and pulled out a flannel jacket.

"Daniel's favorite jacket. I wondered what had happened to this." Emma pulled it close and rubbed it against her cheek, then slipped it over her shoulders. At the funeral, they'd received a box of Daniel's personal items from his police locker, but this wasn't included. It was special, a gift from their parents when he was a teen and worn soft over the years from wear.

"I found it in the break room," Jess explained. "He was always leaving his stuff everywhere. Maybe I shouldn't have taken it, but I thought your family would want to have it."

Emma burrowed her chin in the collar and inhaled. She could still smell Daniel. "I will absolutely treasure this. I'm not even sure what to say." She stood and reached across the table and gave Jess a hug. "Thank you."

"He was a good officer. Relentless in pursuing the truth."

Just one more way that we were exactly alike.

"But not arrogant like some of the guys get. He never let the power of being a cop go to his head. He was kind and fair to everyone."

It wasn't surprising that Daniel was well thought of at work, but still, it was good to hear it from Jess.

"Did you know that he was investigating an old case?" Emma asked.

Jess's eyes narrowed. "You mean Jack Murray's murder?"

Emma trod carefully. "Yeah. Did he talk to you about it?"

"He said something about it a while back, then never really brought it up again. I thought maybe he'd given up on it. The murder happened a long time ago. Why are you asking? Did Danny discuss it with you?"

"No. Not really. He mentioned it once over the phone. It seemed important to him, though. Did you live around here back then?"

"Yeah, but I was in high school. I remember people talking about it, mostly because the Murrays were a big family in town. But it didn't really affect me. I was busy doing the usual teen stuff and, well, it wasn't like we knew the Murrays." She stabbed her straw into her drink a few times, then added, "I overheard you talking to Pruitt yesterday. You don't believe your brother was killed randomly in that traffic stop?"

"No, I don't."

She sat back, her lips pressing into a thin line. "There's something you should know. After it happened, I was the first on the scene."

Emma straightened. "You were there? Did he say anything to you?"

"No. I'm sorry." She picked at her napkin. "This is so difficult. I think about this all the time and wonder if there was something more I could have done for him, but when I got there, he was unconscious and... Anyway, the ambulance got there, and they took him away. I found out later that he had died at the hospital." Her voice broke, and she swiped at her cheek and looked at a wide-banded sports watch on her wrist. "I'm late for work. This didn't turn out the way I meant. I'm sorry. I wanted to meet with you to tell you a few stories about Danny, maybe give you some comfort, but I've ended up crying."

"No. No, it's okay. Really. And I'd love to get together again sometime." She touched her fingers to the jacket. "Thanks again for this. It's so thoughtful of you."

Jess reached across the table and squeezed her hand. "Absolutely. I thought so much of Danny, and I want to be here for you."

This prison's visiting room was like others Emma had been in, with a counter running along a wall of windows, each separated with a divider for privacy. She sat on her side of the fingerprint-smudged glass waiting for Mink to be brought into the visitors' room, a mix of anxiety and determination coursing through her. Interviewing was her strength. She loved the challenge of getting someone to open up to her, and then picking their brain for information, discovering something new, a key fact that made the story.

What she didn't love was this sticky brown stuff smeared on the countertop in front of her. She kept her elbows and hands to her sides and eyed the red phone hanging on the wall, dreading placing it near her face. If only she could have brought in her purse, with her packet of clean wipes. She looked around the room for a hand sanitizer dispenser, found none and got caught up in checking out the other visitors, their conversations filling the air with a variety of emotions: joy, anger, sadness, boredom.

Two chairs down, a woman bounced a fussy toddler on the counter while his tiny fists banged on the glass, saying, "Da Da." Emma's heart went out to the woman. Getting in here to visit was no easy feat. Emma thought of what she'd gone through, being searched, questioned, stripped of her belongings and escorted by a stone-faced guard through the gatehouse, and she didn't even have a kid in tow.

A noise drew her back to her own window, where Mink appeared and settled into the chair on the other side. She inhaled stale air and shook off her nerves, uncertain what to expect. She'd researched him, but there was very little online. The one photo she'd found was of a young, scared guy in handcuffs being led into the courthouse. Nothing like the man who sat in front of her now, who was wiry thin, with dark slicked-back hair and a face full of sharp features, all except for his eyes, which were round and soft brown and stared at her quizzically.

Emma scooted forward and reached for the phone. Mink did the same and spoke first. "Do I know you?"

"No. We've never met. I'm Emma Hayes. I came here to ask some questions about Jack Murray's murder."

His expression changed. "Don't want to discuss it," he said, reaching forward to hang up the phone.

"Wait!" Emma pounced at the window, tapping it with her hand, giving him her best pleading look. He put the phone back to his ear. "Please hear me out," she said. "It's important."

"Why do you want to know about Murray?"

"I'm not with the police. I'm an investigative journalist."

His brows shot up. "You're going to write a story about Murray's murder?"

"No. Not exactly."

"If you're not going to write about Murray's murder, what are you here for?"

In her whole career, Emma had never lied to get information. She wasn't going to start now. "It's more personal than an assignment. My brother was with the county sheriff's office and had reopened Jack Murray's case and—"

"That's what looks familiar about you. You look like him."

Dread shuddered through her. "You met Daniel?"

"Yes. A few weeks ago, on a Wednesday, I believe."

"Wednesday the fifth?"

"Maybe. Couldn't say for sure. But he came here to interview me. Just like you're doing now. So, you're wasting your time. And mine. Whatever you need to know, you should talk—"

"My brother is dead."

The words hung in the air between them. He sat back and regarded her with a compassionate expression that hinted at inner strength and kindness. Emma could see remnants of what Kate must have found attractive in him all those years ago.

"I'm sorry," he finally said.

Emma pushed aside her emotions and continued, "They told me that he was killed in the line of duty during a traffic stop, but I don't believe that. Before he was killed, he called me about an old case he was investigating. He didn't go into detail over the phone. I was on my way to River Falls to talk to him when we got word of his death."

"You think he was killed because he was digging into the Murray case?"

"Yes, I do. And someone is after me now. They must think I know something. But I don't."

"That's why you're here."

"Yes."

"I wanted to help your brother, but I didn't have anything new to tell him."

"You know Jake Crawford?"

He tilted his head back and laughed. "Oh, yeah. I know the guy. He's the reason I'm in here."

"Crawford was shot."

Mink leaned forward. "Shot? Is he still alive?"

"Barely. I was talking to him when it happened. Right before the bullet hit, he said your name."

Mink lowered his gaze and shook his head.

Visiting was limited to twenty minutes, and Emma felt time slipping away. "Jack Murray—"

"I didn't kill him. But I'm sure you don't believe that. I don't think your brother did, either. Not that it matters at this point. I'm really done discussing this. There's nothing new to tell, and nothing is going to change the fact that I'm here for something I didn't do."

In her experience with interviewing prisoners, Emma found that some were angry, some belligerent, and many simply dulled, like they'd been beaten down and lost hope. Her impression of Mink was different. He seemed resigned to his fate, even at peace with it. "At least tell me your side of the story. I'm trying to figure out what happened to my brother, that's all, and I need your help."

He swiped his nose and ran his finger on the leg of his orange jumpsuit. "We mostly talked about that day. I told him about a fight between my girlfriend and me and that I went out with Crawford to drown my sorrows. Keep in mind, we were only nineteen at the time. Anyway, Crawford found a case of beer at his dad's place. We started with that, got loosened up, then decided we needed more. We weren't legal, so we tried to lift a bottle of Jack Daniel's from the shelf at Buck's, that gas station store on the west side of town. Is it still there?"

"I don't know. I'm not from here."

"Oh…well, anyway, we hooded up, wore sunglasses, like the stupid morons we were. And the guy behind the counter busted us right away. Told us he was going to call the cops. Crawford, the idiot, pushed the guy down and we ran. No one got hurt, but he ended up taking the booze and a wad of cash from the register."

"Assault and robbery."

He nodded. "Yeah. But not murder. There were security cameras at the gas station. I remember seeing them. About three in the morning, the cops came by the house. I was passed out drunk. Don't even remember getting home. But I was sure they'd come for me because of the robbery, but they arrested me for murder. I couldn't figure it out. I had no idea Murray was even dead until the cops told me."

"They never questioned you about the robbery?"

"No. I fessed up, though. Told them to talk to the gas station owner. Told my attorney, too. Nothing ever came of it."

"Who was your attorney?"

"His name was Salieri. David, I think."

Emma made a quick note.

"He was just some guy the court gave me. I never heard from him again after sentencing." He swiped his nose again, sniffed a few times, cleared his throat. "The thing is, no one would have wanted Jack Murray dead. He was a great guy. Everyone liked him. Guess he was killed over money, so…"

"Who else worked the stables besides you and Kate and would have known about the cash in the safe?"

"Everyone who worked there knew about it. Half the jobs were paid out in cash." He rolled his eyes to the ceiling. "Delivery guys were in and out all the time, and let's see, there was a trainer and several jockeys. The jockeys mostly came in and trained in the mornings. Your brother asked me about them, but I couldn't remember any of their names. It could have been one of them, if they were looking for quick money. I don't think they made much racing. But like I said, a lot of people came through there."

"What about the trainer? What was his name?"

"Banks. I don't remember his first name. I only maybe talked to him a couple times. Ask me, he didn't know how to do his job. Left most of the training and scheduling up to the jockeys."

Banks? She'd heard someone say that the other day in the barn. So it was a name? She jotted down a few notes, then said, "The robbery only accounts for a short time. You could have robbed the gas station and then gone out to the farm and killed Murray for the extra cash. You must have known it was in the safe."

"No. No, that's not what happened. We stole the liquor and cash and then picked up this girl that Crawford knew and continued our binge. We pretty much partied the rest of the night."

Emma stared at him. Waiting.

"I told the cops all this back then. The convenience store robbery was never pinned on us, and Crawford wasn't going to come forward with any information. He'd rather see me go to prison for murder than implicate himself in a crime."

"What about the girl you picked up?"

"I have no idea who she was. Some girl Crawford had the hots for. Didn't matter. He denied everything, even partying with the girl. None of it came out in the trial. Or ever." He sighed. "Look, I didn't do it. I know they found the shotgun in the back seat of my car, but I didn't do it. I was an easy target. I'd gotten in trouble before and had a record, but all that was kid stuff. What Crawford and I did, stealing that liquor, was wrong and stupid, but I've more than paid for that crime."

Emma switched gears. "You said you had a fight with Kate earlier that day."

He squinted. "No, I didn't. I said I had a fight with my girlfriend. I didn't mention her name was Kate. You've done your homework. Who all have you talked to about this?"

"Kate's brother and sister."

He grew quiet at the mention of Logan and Rachel.

"The Greers have lived a long time without knowing what happened to Kate," Emma said. "Most people around here speculated that she was in on it with you, and when you got busted, she ran with the money."

"Everyone's wrong about that. Kate wasn't capable of murder. She was there and got herself killed because she saw what happened to Murray. She was a witness."

"Maybe she witnessed you killing him."

"No." His eyes flashed with anger, but his voice remained calm.

"Rachel overheard you two fighting on the phone the day Jack Murray was killed. What was that all about?"

He frowned. "I don't like what you're getting at. I would have never hurt—"

"But you two did have a fight."

"Yeah, we had a fight. I'm not denying it. The whole thing was my fault. I was being selfish. We had plans to go to a concert that Saturday in Franklin, but she was all worked up about a foal that'd died. They were burying it that afternoon, and she wanted to be there. That was it. That's all there was to it. A stupid fight between kids."

The guard approached. "Let's go, Mink. Time's up."

Mink stood but kept the phone to his ear. "I should have been with her that day. She may still be alive if I had. I regret our fight, how I acted, the things I said. And I've had to live with that. But I didn't hurt Kate. I would never have hurt her. I loved her. Still do."

"Is there anything you need? Anything I can do for you?" Logan held the phone to his ear as he scanned the other cars in the prison parking lot, making sure they weren't followed.

"It's so good of you to call and check on me," Lillian said. Her voice sounded strong. "But I'm fine, really. I'm back home, and Seth is taking good care of me."

"I'm glad to hear that. I feel bad about what happened. I'm sorry if anything I said—"

"Please, there's no need to apologize. The conversation was upsetting, but you didn't cause my collapse. My heart gets credit for that. And me. I've been stubborn about getting a pacemaker put in, and my arrhythmia is worse. This was my wake-up call."

"You're always doing for others," Logan said. "You need to take better care of yourself."

"The fundraiser is still on, by the way. I'm going to work on the guest list today. I thought we should invite that new—"

"Lillian! Stop." He laughed. "I'm not worried about the fundraiser. I'm worried about you. Please promise me that you'll slow down and rest."

"Okay, okay. I get it. Rest. I will. I promise."

Emma exited the front doors of the prison. "I've got to go, Lillian, but I'll call back and check on you later." He wrapped up the call and pocketed his phone, his eyes never leaving Emma as she crossed the parking lot. Her stride was purposeful and confident, her red hair bouncing on her shoulders. If he was honest, he was completely captivated by her. She was beautiful, kind, smart...but it was more than that. She possessed something that drew him to her. It'd taken him a while to figure it out, but he now realized that it was her strength. Despite everything she'd gone through, she remained strong. And that inner strength was what he found most attractive about her.

She climbed into the passenger seat and burrowed into her brother's flannel jacket that Deputy Davis had given her. Logan adjusted the heat. "How'd it go?"

"Well, it wasn't a complete waste of time," she said. "I got a name. Banks. After Lillian collapsed and I went to get Seth, I heard talking in the barn and the word *Banks*. Turns out he was a trainer at the stable. Mink didn't care for him. He said he did little to actually train the horses."

"And you think Mink is a good judge of character?"

She ignored his sarcasm and went on about Mink's alibi. "Mink said that he and Crawford robbed a convenience store, and then picked up a girl Crawford knew and partied the rest of the night."

"What girl? And why didn't all that come out at the trial?"

"He can't remember the girl's name. But he said that he told the police and his attorney about her, and no one pursued it."

"Maybe he did. I didn't pay that close attention—it was such a horrible time for our family. But the newspapers and media made it seem like a tight case. Evidence was found in Mink's car and—"

"Planted, he claims."

"That's what they all say."

"What if he's telling the truth?" She turned in her seat and directly faced him. Suddenly the Range Rover seemed smaller. And he didn't mind, not a bit. "In Daniel's note-book," she went on, "it looked like he had arrested Craw-ford. Maybe Crawford made a deal and gave up some info on the night Murray was murdered. Mink said that Daniel came to see him. I checked the visitor logs. It was Wednes-day the fifth, two days after Daniel arrested Crawford and one day before Daniel was murdered."

"The timing is right. But there's nothing about his visit with Mink in the notebook. Don't you find that strange?"

"Yeah. Unless he didn't have time to record it." She took out her phone and began scrolling through the photos she'd taken of Daniel's notebook. "If what Mink says is true, al-most everyone would have had to have been crooked. The police, the attorney. Mink said his name was Salieri. You ever heard of him?"

"No. We'll have to look him up." Logan drew in a deep breath. "Mink's almost thirty now. If he was wrongly im-prisoned, he's lost some of the best years of his life."

Emma turned back around and put her seat belt on. "I can't even begin to wrap my mind around what it'd be like to be in prison for something you didn't do."

Silence settled between them as Logan put the vehicle into gear and headed toward the road to River Falls. He thought back about Mink and how judgmental he'd been of him. He didn't want his sister going out with him because he had a bad reputation. But what did he really know about him? Only what he'd heard. He never took the time to get to know the guy. Kate must have seen something in him, or she never would have dated him.

"Do you remember when Seth started making money on his horses?"

"Not exactly. He had a few big wins in a row from one horse, King's Spirit. He did the full circuit and then used him as a sire, I believe. Kate once told me that she was never allowed near the horse. It had a special team." Logan turned onto the main road. A dark flash of color in his rearview mirror caught his eye. A black SUV had appeared on the horizon behind them.

"Mink was insistent that Kate had nothing to do with Jack Murray's murder," Emma said. Logan kept one eye on the SUV. It was getting closer. He increased his own speed, while Emma kept talking. "My gut instinct is that Mink didn't have anything to do with it, either. I can't prove that, but…"

The SUV had faded in the rearview mirror. Logan breathed a sigh of relief, eased up on the accelerator and looked over at Emma. She was still scrolling through the notebook pages she'd photographed, her brows knitted together. "What is it? Have you found something?" he asked, glancing at her phone's screen.

"Daniel's notes on an accident he investigated. These numbers are strange. I wonder if— Watch out!"

Emma's scream filled the air as the SUV rammed them in the side. The Range Rover veered to the left, one tire dropping off the road. The wheel shuddered as he overcorrected and swerved into the other lane. He cranked the wheel to the right, tires squealing, Emma screaming and— Bam! Metal crunched as the car now rammed them from behind. His shoulder slammed against the door, and hot pain radiated through his body. He gripped the wheel tighter, floored the accelerator and shot forward.

Emma hung on to the dash with both hands as the speedometer steadily climbed and the car careened. "We're going too fast."

Logan dared a glance in the mirror. The SUV's grille loomed inches from his bumper. If they went off the road out here, they'd be sitting targets.

He accelerated, the Range Rover rattled, the steering wheel shimmied, but he kept his focus forward— Bam! The wheel was torn from his grip, the vehicle spiraled and the cab filled with Emma's cries. Panic shot through him as they hit the ditch.

NINE

Logan fought to open his eyes, to swim to the surface of the swirling darkness in his mind. Somewhere, faded and far away, he heard the metallic popping and scraping of the Range Rover's passenger door being pried open. Cool air swept through the vehicle's cabin and over his body, and he heard Emma's muffled voice. He tried to reach for her, but his arm was heavy and tired. He prayed—*God, please let her be okay*—but soon his prayers faded from his lips, and he sank back into the darkness.

He woke again and this time managed to open his eyes. He was pressed against the steering wheel, and shards of glass covered his body. The airbag hung limp like a deflated balloon. Memories flooded his mind: the SUV barreling down on them, then disappearing, a sense of relief, followed by the sudden impact and piercing screams, the jolt to his body as they hit the ditch, Emma's voice... *Emma?* He turned in his seat, hot pain searing through his neck muscles. Fear overtook him as he fought to free himself from the seat belt. Emma was gone!

Then footsteps outside. Someone was approaching the car. "Help me. I'm in here. Help—" He went mute with terror. Help, or the man who ran them off the road? He twisted under the constraints of the seat belt and fumbled with the clasp, fear-infused adrenaline pumping through his body. The belt was stuck. *Come on, open, open...* The footsteps stopped outside his window.

He rolled his gaze upward and saw not a friendly face, nor a helpful hand, but the cold black barrel of a gun. His heart thumped in his throat as he squeezed his eyes closed and waited for the click of the trigger, the blast of the bullet, the impact. Would he feel any pain? Would he see God right away? But instead, the wheezing sound of a semi's air brakes filled the air, and a man's voice called out, "Hey, what's going on? What are you doing? Hey!"

Logan opened his eyes and caught a flash of a dark jacket as the man with the gun turned and ran.

"Hey, stop!" the voice yelled again.

A car door slammed, tires screeched on asphalt and an engine roared away. Logan worked at his seat belt again. The strap squeezed his midsection, and his swollen, clumsy fingers were no use as he tried to release the clasp.

"Are you okay?"

His head jerked up. A man peered at him through the shattered window. Not the man with the gun. This man was burly, with a tan coat bearing a trucking emblem and a friendly face.

"We were forced off the road," Logan said. "And...do you see a woman out there?" Was Emma thrown from the car and lying hurt on the road?

"There's no woman out here. Hold on—I'll get you out."

The trucker yanked on the door several times. Finally, it popped open with a loud metal cracking sound. He worked the seat belt over, trying to get it to release, then pulled a knife from the side pocket of his pants, released the blade and sawed at the belt.

As soon as he was free, Logan climbed out of the wreckage and slowly moved around the outside of the Range Rover, scanning the ditch where they had landed. His brain knocked in his skull, and every muscle in his body screamed with soreness, but he had to find Emma. Did she fly through the window? He thought she was wearing her seat belt, but he couldn't be sure, and she was nowhere to be seen on the weed-strewn ground. He looked at the road just slightly above him and saw only the semitruck where this Good Samaritan had jumped out to help him. No other cars. No sign of Emma.

"Take it easy, buddy," the trucker said. "You could be hurt. What's your name?"

"Logan. Logan Greer."

"I'm Jerry. You should sit down. You've been in a major accident here."

"I can't. I need to find Emma."

"Emma?"

Logan stopped searching. "Tell me what you saw when you pulled up."

"All I saw was a guy pointing a gun at your window. I yelled at him, and he took off running. He got into a dark gray, no, I think it was black, yeah, a black SUV and peeled out of here. I didn't even get a look at his face. He was wearing a hood and sunglasses. Hey, there's blood on—"

"Was there a woman in his car?"

"Don't know. Sorry. It happened fast, and his windows were tinted."

Logan's nerves danced over his skin. He raked at his hair, feeling a lump in the middle of his forehead where he'd hit the steering wheel. His stomach rolled and he felt a wave of dizziness wash over him. The sirens wailing in the distance kept tempo with the pounding in his head.

The semi driver motioned to the ground. "Here, sit down,

buddy. You're looking a little white around the gills. Hear those sirens? The ambulance ain't too far now."

"No. No ambulance. Please. I've got to find my friend. She's in danger." Emma had been in the car with him. He remembered the sound of the door being pried open and heard her moaning. She was alive. At least at that point. But for how long? The driver of the SUV ran them off the road on purpose, with a plan to kill him and take Emma. Now time was ticking away.

He fished his phone out of his pocket, shaky fingers pushing the numbers on the screen. Joe answered right away.

"It's Emma," Logan said. "She's been abducted. I need help."

Emma opened her eyes to darkness, her hands bound above her head and her legs stretched and tied at the ankles. Her tongue swelled, her mouth tasted sticky and dry, and her lips were crusted with coppery-tasting blood. *Where am I? Why am I tied—* Tiny prickles skittered over her cheek—a spider!

She thrashed her head back and forth, the concrete floor scratching at her skin, only to send the spider scurrying into her hairline, close to her ear. She twisted her head to the side to smash the spider, feeling the smear of it on her scalp. Her heart thudded. The coldness of a concrete floor soaked through her clothes and went straight to her bones. She realized she was in a basement or a cellar. But why? She remembered the SUV forcing them off the road, and the wreck, Logan… He had to be okay. Was he here, too? "Logan. Logan?" The words were a dry hiss on her tongue.

She strained her eyes, looking for a shaft of light, and her ears, listening for any sounds, and detected a faint scurrying sound from somewhere nearby. Could Logan be nearby but unconscious? Or could her abductor be here, watching her? Fear seized her, but she saw nothing and only heard the *plunk, plunk* of a slow drip echoing off the walls, the wind blowing outside rhythmically like ocean waves and that scurrying sound. *What is it?* It grew louder. *Finger-nails scratching over bricks? Logan?*

Something warm brushed against her leg and set off a fresh surge of panic. She screamed and yanked at her ties, bucked her hips, kicked her feet. *Rats, no...no... Oh, God, help me.* Her heart raced and adrenaline pounded through her veins. *Help me*, she prayed, her pleas filling her mind, her heart, then mixed with sobs as she cried out, "Help me! Help me!"

A high-pitched screech filled the air, and then a loud boom and the reverberation of metal—the sound of a cel-lar door being opened. A sword of light pierced the dark-ness, sending the rats running for cover, and revealing swatches of the damp earthen walls and the blackened, gnarled wooden beams of a cellar, where she now realized she, alone, had been bound. She strained against the ropes and was able to twist her head and look past the trailing spiderwebs that glistened in the narrow shaft of light. At the top of the cellar stairs, a dark figure loomed shadowy against the daylight.

"Hello, darlin'." His voice was low and guttural. "It's time you and me had a little talk."

Despite the pain spreading over his skull, Logan paced back and forth. The Range Rover was crumpled and man-gled and tilted half-upside-down in the ditch. Totaled. What would Huey say? And where was Joe? He'd called him over thirty minutes ago. Who knew what was happening to Emma at this very second? And here he was, stuck answering Pruitt's questions. He needed to get out of here and look for Emma. The thought of her being harmed sent a rage through him like he'd never felt before.

He turned on Pruitt. "What are you doing to find Emma?"

Pruitt flinched, but his expression quickly turned sympathetic. "Every deputy in the county is looking for that SUV. Choppers are heading out, too. And we're setting up roadblocks on the major roads."

"What about side roads, and forest service roads, and—"

"I'm doing what I can. We don't have enough manpower to cover everything." He eased up and shook his head. "I know you're worried. But I've got to ask these questions. Something you tell me might help us find her. Now, did you see anything or notice anything about the guy with the gun?"

"No. I just saw the gun that was pointed at my head." How could he not have seen the guy's face, or his eyes, or anything about him? "Wait. He had a dark jacket. I remember the jacket, but that's all."

Pruitt took out a notepad and pointed his pen at the wreckage. "Whose vehicle is this?"

"It belongs to my friend Huey. He loaned it to us."

"And you said you first noticed the SUV about a mile back. Why were you out here? Where were you going?"

How much should I tell Pruitt?

Pruitt scowled. "I can't help you if you don't give me some information. Are you holding something back?"

"We were going home. But we'd been at the prison."

"The prison?"

"Yeah. That's right. Emma wanted to talk to Michael Kincaid about the case."

Pruitt stopped writing. "Mink? Did she get anything from him?"

Logan should give up Banks's name, but could he really trust Pruitt? Daniel obviously hadn't trusted someone in the sheriff's department. "I didn't get much of a chance to find out. We didn't get far down the road before I noticed the SUV in my mirror."

Pruitt let out a long sigh and waved the other deputy over. "Put in a call to the warden and let them know we'd like to see their parking lot security footage. And I want to see the visitor logs for the last month." The deputy stepped aside to make the call, and Pruitt turned back to Logan. "It's possible the SUV followed you from the prison. If it shows up on security, we might be able to get a plate number and owner registration."

"Let's hope so." A red car appeared on the horizon. Logan broke away from Pruitt and started that way. "My ride's here. I'm leaving."

"Not until we've finished. I've got more questions."

"They'll have to wait. I need to find Emma." Logan kept going. Let Pruitt try to stop him.

"Banks," Logan told Joe as soon as he was in the car. He strapped on his seat belt right away and squeezed his eyes against the pounding in his head.

"Banks?"

"Banks is the name we're looking for. It's the name of a trainer Seth was using around the time Jack was killed. Mink mentioned him to Emma as a possible suspect. That's the only thing I've got to go on." He punched the name into the search engine on his phone. Nothing came up. "I can't get service out here."

"Did you tell Pruitt about Banks?"

"No. I was going to. Maybe I should have. I don't know, but… Ugh…not a single bar on here." His gut had told him not to tell Pruitt about Banks, but what if his gut was wrong?

"Let me drive up the road a way. This might just be a dead spot. You can call Rachel and have her look on her end for the name Banks."

As they drove, Logan filled him in on the SUV and the guy with the gun. "I swear, the guy was this close to pulling the trigger. I'd be dead now, if it weren't for the semi driver." Too many things were happening—he could hardly process it all. He only knew that he didn't want this guy anywhere near Emma. "We've got to find her before he kills her."

"We will. Don't lose hope, okay?"

They crested a hill, and bars popped up on Logan's screen. He dialed Rachel and quickly told her what they needed. She promised to get back to him as soon as she had something.

He disconnected and turned back to Joe. "I told Pruitt we'd come from talking to Mink when we were run off the road, but my gut instinct told me not to tell him about Banks. I don't know if I did the right thing. I don't even know what the right thing is anymore." He looked ahead and pointed out a small gravel road that forked off the main road. "Try that one."

Joe took a hard right. "You're doing everything you can, buddy."

Joe's Impala bounced along the country roads. Logan's head ached with every bump, and waves of nausea swarmed his gut. A concussion, probably. His adrenaline drained from his body, leaving him suddenly exhausted. He grew quiet, checking his phone every five minutes, waiting for Rachel to get back to them.

Still, after two hours of searching, they'd come up empty. "It's like he just disappeared."

Logan brushed his fingers over the bump on his fore-head and winced. "This is impossible. He could have taken her anywhere."

"Disappearing isn't all that hard up here. There are thousands of acres of woodland with forest service roads and hollers and draws."

"I don't know what I'll do if she's..." Logan couldn't say it out loud.

Joe maneuvered his car down the mountain's switch-backs. "Pray, buddy. Ask for God's guidance."

Logan prayed silently as they continued to search the roadside. They passed by dilapidated houses and barns, looking in vain for signs of a black SUV. Every second that ticked away narrowed their chances of finding Emma alive. Logan remembered what she felt like in his arms. The softness of her hair against his face. And her smell...like warm flowers and sunshine. He should have held on tighter, insisted that she give up this quest she was on. Rachel was right. They had no business going to the prison today. If the worst had happened to Emma, he would never forgive himself.

TEN

"Where is it?" he demanded.

Cold dread embalmed Emma. She was helpless, her body immobilized and completely at this man's mercy. "Where... where is what? I don't know what you want."

He snatched her hair and yanked her head closer to his face. In the meager light filtered from the open door above the stairs, all she saw was the gleam of his eyes. His breath came in sour, hot spurts on her cheek. "Don't mess with me, lady, or I'll kill you right now."

"Please, I don't know anything. I swear." She heard the flick of a knife blade, and the cold, sharp edge of steel slid along her neck. Frantically she searched her mind for the right answer, something that would make him stop. "All I had was his notebook, but there was nothing in it." Her voice was small, tiny, scared.

"You'll have to do better than that. I know he told you more."

"No. He didn't have a chance. All I've got is the—"

The tip of the blade, tiny and razor-like, pierced the skin under her ear.

She whimpered.

"You're lying."

"No. I...I'm telling you the truth."

He let go of her head and relief flooded through her, and she felt a second of respite from the pain before his hand came down hard on her face. The sting reverberated through her, and blood oozed over her tongue. She turned away, trembling and praying that he wouldn't hit her again.

"Tell me," he repeated, his voice eerily calm as he traced the blade of the knife down her cheek to the hollow of her neck and back to her ear.

She held her breath, afraid to even swallow. Every inch of her hummed with fear. *Please, God, please. I want to live.*

"Do you hear the rats?" A dry, phlegmy cough racked his chest and the blade bounced over her skin. The air reeked of this evil man. "Huh? Do you hear them?"

"Yes." Tears streamed down her cheeks.

His thumb and forefinger cupped her jaw and tipped her face upward until she was forced to stare into his eyes. "You're playing games now, but a few hours alone with these rats and you'll be ready to talk."

She felt blood trickle down her neck where the blade had cut her skin. It mixed with her tears and soaked into her hair. Memories flashed through her mind: Daniel's quirky laugh and childhood games in the woods, the warm sun on her face, her mother's voice calling them home for supper... *Mama*... She thought of her mother and father, losing two children and how heartbroken they would be, and she pleaded with her captor, begged him to spare her. "Please don't leave me here. My parents, my parents—"

Her pleas were stopped short by the sound of tape being ripped off a roll. "Wait. No, please, listen to me." Her whole body shook. "I'm telling you the truth. I..." But the tape hit her open lips, sticking to her teeth, her tongue. A bitter, chemical taste filled her mouth. She gagged, her muffled cries echoing in the glum as his footsteps retreated and the cellar door slammed behind him, leaving her in darkness. An engine roared, and tires crunched on gravel as he drove away. *Don't leave me*, a tiny voice in her head cried.

Then she heard the faint echo of scurrying claws.

Rachel finally called. She had an address. "I found it listed in the county tax records. The owner of the property is Arlo Banks. I searched everywhere, and it's the only reference to anyone by the name of Banks that I could find for this county."

Twenty minutes later, they parked Joe's car along the road, partially hidden by an overgrowth of scrub trees, and walked through the woods to the back of the house, hoping to avoid detection. Their shoes kicked up leaves as they walked, filling the air with a damp, moldy smell.

Joe moved ahead, his shoulders rounded in a worried slouch. "I don't like this," he said. "It's isolated out here. We don't know the lay of the land. We're vulnerable. If something goes wrong, the only person who knows where we might be is Rachel. Even if she calls Pruitt, it'll take the cops forever to find us. We should call them, maybe wait for them before we go at this alone."

"There's not enough time. We just need to keep our wits—There!" The top of the house appeared over the trees. They crouched as they got closer and squatted in the weeds, surveying the area, checking for any signs of Emma or Banks.

At one time, the farmhouse might have been picturesque, Logan thought. It had a deep front porch, several outbuildings, a barn and fenced pastures. But the home was weathered, the roof sagged, the once whitewashed clapboards were stripped by years of rain and wind. The barn wasn't in any better shape. It shrugged to one side, half the roof missing. The pastures were empty and overgrown, and weeds licked at the base of the outbuildings, making them almost inaccessible.

"Looks like it's been abandoned for years," Joe said. "I don't think she's here."

But she *was* here. Logan was sure of it. As if somehow his heart could feel her presence. Which sounded foolish, but it was true. Not that he'd say anything like that out loud. "Maybe not, but let's check it out anyway. You take the outbuildings. I've got the house." He headed for the pasture.

Joe started after him, then called out, "Wait!" He pointed to a spot a few yards away. "Those look like tire tracks."

Logan stooped down to examine the ruts. "You're right. And they haven't been here for long. They're still well-defined." His heart kicked up a notch. He knew it. He knew she was here. He pointed to a metal-sided outbuilding, partially concealed with trees and barely visible from where they stood. "Looks like they lead back there. Come on."

Logan's thoughts ran the gamut as they raced toward the outbuilding. *We've found her! What has he done to her? Is she alive?* The siding was rusting along the seams and fastenings, and the base of the building was choked out by weeds. There were no windows, only a small door next to a padlocked single-car garage door.

Joe tried the knob. "It's locked."

Logan pushed past Joe and shook the knob. Then he stepped back and cocked his leg, smashing the heel of his boot against the door. Pain shot through his hip and up his spine, but he kicked again and again, a fog of anger and fear taking over his senses.

"What are you doing, man? This isn't right!"

"She might be in here."

"You don't know that. You can't just break into someone's property."

Watch me. Logan was in a different world, one filled with past trauma and frustration and helplessness, and his only thought was saving Emma. He kicked the door over and over until it gave way with a loud pop. "Emma!" His voice rang hollow.

The building was empty except for a few boxes stacked on the dirt floor and some rusty tools. No sign of Emma.

Logan leaned over and shook his head, his body exhausted, his breath coming in short spurts. "I thought...I thought she'd be in here."

"It's okay, buddy. We're going to find her." Joe placed his hand on his shoulder.

"What if we don't? I can't lose her. Not like Kate. Not again—"

"Don't let your emotions cloud your thinking. You said it earlier. We've got to keep our wits about us. You need a clear head if you want to help Emma, right?"

Logan straightened. Joe was right. "I'll go check out the house."

"Good idea. I'll take the barn."

They separated. Logan approached the back of the house, scanning the windows for any sign of movement inside. The place was eerily still. He checked the back door, but it was securely boarded. Most of the windows were boarded, too, but he managed to find a small crack between sheets of plywood. He peered through, but the house was completely empty, still, dark, too dark to see much of anything. Over his shoulder, he saw Joe making his way from the barn through the yard toward what looked like an old poultry house. Logan turned back to the cracked board, grabbed hold of the wood and yanked. It gave way, dust and dirt filling the air and sunlight flooding into the interior of the house. He pushed through the opening and stepped inside.

The pungent smell of must and mold crept into his nostrils. He coughed and blinked, trying to adjust his eyes to the dim light, his vision catching on a couple of mice scurrying across the floor. Cobwebs dangled from the ceiling. To his right, a green floral sofa with metal legs was pushed against the wall, a pile of beer cans next to it. Everything was covered in dust and grime. Nothing except bugs and rodents had been in here for a long time. Still, the place had a feel of evil about it. He shook off a shudder and moved toward the stairs.

He stopped. What was that noise? Something…a female voice…coming from the kitchen. Emma! He ran through the house, stopping in the middle of the empty kitchen, straining to hear her voice over the hammering of his heartbeat.

Emma's hair had wicked up blood from her wound and dried against her face, and every scraping sound, every squeak that echoed from the dark corners of the cellar, sent panic surging through her veins. Her nerves had buzzed on high alert, as she'd listened and waited for the rats for what seemed like hours. Now her body had fatigued, and all she wanted was to sink into a deep, blissful sleep. "Stay awake, stay awake, stay awake…" she murmured to herself. If she fell asleep the rats would overcome her.

She struggled against the ropes that bound her hands and feet between two posts, stretching her body like a hammock. Her joints screamed for relief, her back ached, her entire body was racked with pain, and she thought of her Lord and the pain He endured for her, and she wanted to cry out to Him for help, but shame overwhelmed her. She'd been so angry about Daniel, feeling like God had abandoned her. She'd

turned her back on everything she believed. But maybe…
God, I'm sorry. Please—

God? God hasn't been there for you for a long time.
The voice came to her from the dark, an echo of Rachel's
words. She shook her head. *Don't give in to despair,* she
told herself, but more words came: *helpless, abandoned,
left to die.* Anger welled inside her again. God allowed
this. And Daniel's death. And all the terrible, evil things
in the world. Illness, pain, suffering. "Why?" she wanted
to shout, but she couldn't even do that.

Her body was weakening, her mind fuzzy and uncon-
trolled. Beady rodent eyes stared at her in the darkness,
but she didn't care. Not really. She was too tired to care.
Don't sleep, she told herself, *don't sleep,* but exhaustion
claimed her, and she drifted, just to startle awake again.
Something had brushed against the tip of her finger! She
jerked her hand, the ropes cutting into her flesh, as something scuttled away. A rat! What if she'd been bitten? Her
mind reeled. And then more scuttling, a tiny squeak near
her ear, and her heart cried out, *God, help me!*

Tears mixed with dust and ran down her cheeks around
the tape plastered on her lips. She choked on her own spit,
her mind pleading for mercy, and then she heard it, a loud
splintering sound and footsteps overhead. "Help, help me!"
But all that came out were muffled sounds, distant and dry.

Logan continued to listen. It was definitely a woman's
voice, not words, but moans, and they were coming from
underneath the floor. "Emma!" he yelled. "Emma! I hear
you. I'm looking for you."

The cries grew louder and more agitated. *Where are
you?* He searched for a trapdoor in the floor, pushing aside
the heavy wood table. Nothing. *Help me find her, please*

help... A cellar. There must be a cellar under the kitchen. His heart flooded with hope as he backtracked through the house and out the window, calling for Joe as he pushed through the weeds along the foundation of the home.

The cellar entrance was toward the back of the house, with a board slid through the handles, securing the door. "Joe!" he called again. He looked over his shoulder and saw his friend running across the yard. "She's here," Logan yelled. "I've found her. She's here."

Her muffled cries grew more desperate as Logan worked to free the board. Finally, it pushed through. Joe caught up to him, and they lifted the heavy doors, sending light streaming through the underground room. Logan hurried down the steps, tripped near the bottom, his hand flying out to the rough stone wall. He barely caught himself, stumbling off balance into the cellar, but she was there on the floor, her hands and feet stretched in opposite directions and tied to support posts. "Emma!"

He knelt next to her and ripped the tape from her mouth as Joe stood behind him, his eyes searching for any danger lurking in the gloom.

"Logan," she whispered, her swollen lips hardly able to form words.

"I'm here now. It's okay."

Her face was cut and bruised, and dried blood covered her neck and matted her hair. Rage boiled inside him. She was bound, beaten and cut. He'd find the man who'd done this to her and... His mind flashed to a very dark place, somewhere darker than he'd been since wartime. A surge of hatred filled his gut, and the need for revenge threatened to swallow him. He gritted his teeth, unwilling to give in to the evil of more violence. He didn't want to go there. Didn't need to. He was no longer that person, he told himself. He never wanted Emma to know that part of him, the darkness that once lurked inside him.

Joe pulled his knife and sawed through the ropes that held her wrists, all the while Logan whispering, "Thank You, God, thank You." A tiny whimper escaped her lips. Joe freed her legs, too, and Logan scooped her up, pulling her close and holding her.

Joe's hand touched his shoulder. "Let's get her out of here."

Logan nodded and carried her up the steps. Outside in the bright light she looked even worse. He placed her gently on the ground, pulling the flannel jacket tighter around her shoulders.

Joe knelt next to them. "Emma, can you hear us? Emma?"

She rolled her eyes open. "You found me. I can't believe you found me." Her small voice was washed in pain and exhaustion.

Logan wanted to pull her close and hold her forever. "I would never have stopped looking...never."

A faint smile appeared on her lips. "I knew that."

The rush of relief he felt was something he wouldn't forget. He looked up at Joe. "We'll need to get her to the ER and have her checked over." Then to Emma, "Can you walk?"

"I think so." She pulled herself to a sitting position. "He told me that he'd be back."

Logan and Joe exchanged a look. Emma continued, "He wanted something from me, but I don't know what. He kept asking me where it was. Then he'd hit me when I couldn't tell him...but I had no idea what he wanted and... I was so scared. I asked God for help. I prayed. And you came."

Logan didn't hold back. He pulled her close, his lips brushing the top of her head. "I'm sorry. I'm so sorry this happened to you. I'm here now and you're okay. He'll never hurt you again, I promise."

"We should call an ambulance," Joe said.

Logan looked up at his friend. "It'll take first responders a half hour to get out here. It might be faster to transport her there ourselves."

Joe agreed. "I'll go get the car." He started to backtrack across the yard.

Emma clutched her head and grew paler. Her body swayed. Logan slipped his arm around her waist to steady her. He stopped and tenderly cupped her face, pulling her close, their foreheads touching. "I thought I'd lost you. I was frantic. I would never forgive myself if something happened to you." He traced his thumb down her cheek and slid it over her lips. "Emma, I'm..."

A noise drew his attention. He turned to see the black SUV sitting in the lane, its engine idling, spots of sunlight glinting off its tinted windshield.

Emma's body trembled against his, and she cried out, "He's back!"

ELEVEN

Emma screamed again as the driver gunned the engine. She heard Joe yelling for them to run for the trees, but she stood rooted in fear, her heart pounding, her muscles locked in panic, her mind weary and muddled.

Logan snatched her arm and yanked her from her trance, dragging her toward the trees at the edge of the property. "Run, Emma. Run!"

Her legs, heavy and cumbersome, floundered, like she was moving through thick water. Her whole world had slowed. Except the SUV. It was speeding right toward them. "He's going to hit us!" she yelled.

Logan clenched her hand and pulled her along. "Don't look back!"

She turned her focus forward and willed her body to co-operate. Thistles clawed at her legs and scraped her arms as they raced through the field. Behind them, wheels pounded the dirt, crunching weeds, spitting out stones and kicking up dust that clouded the air. Her lungs burned, and her legs ached as she and Logan reached the trees and burst into the safety of the woods. They kept running, continuing deeper into the shelter of the trees, her feet tripping over roots and fallen branches.

Finally, they stopped, and Emma doubled over, sucking

air into her lungs and gagging as acid burned through her depleted stomach. Her mouth was bone-dry, her tongue like tacky glue, and her head spun. When was the last time she ate or drank water? Her body quivered, ready to give out. She lifted her gaze and saw Logan and Joe standing nearby, busy scanning the woods. Infinite gratitude for these two men and for her answered prayers threatened to drain her last bit of energy, but she couldn't give in to her weakness.

"I don't think he followed us," Joe said. "It's less than ten minutes to my car from here. We need to get moving again." They both looked over at Emma.

She took another deep breath and straightened. "I can make it." She hoped that was true.

They moved through the trees at a slower pace, but she still lagged. At one point, Logan slipped his arm around her. She'd noticed a swollen bruise on his forehead. The accident? Had he been injured?

She leaned close to him, wishing she could melt into the safety of his arms. She pushed back her feelings. Now wasn't the time. Maybe there would never be a time. Her work was in DC, and he was tied to his clinic, and... Why was she thinking about all this? *I'm just lucky to be alive.*

"My car's just ahead," she heard Joe say.

Relief flooded through her. They'd made it.

Logan smiled her way and took her hand, leading her forward. Maybe that was all this could be...a hand of friendship and support when she needed it most. And, if that was all it could be, wasn't that enough?

As soon as they were within cell range, they called the sheriff's office and made a report. Pruitt seemed on top of things, sending out a crew to investigate the abandoned property and a deputy to take her full statement.

Logan rushed her to the ER, where a nurse tended to them. Emma cleaned up in the examination room sink and was checked over. She had bruises and a black eye now to go with the sutures in her shoulder. The cut on her cheek was shallow and required only cleaning and butterfly bandages, plus she was assured that there should be little scarring. Overall, she was lucky that it was nothing more serious. Logan was lucky, too. His head injury turned out to be superficial. No concussion. Deputy Davis came to the hospital and interviewed them. Unfortunately, Emma was unable to provide much of a description of her assailant, other than he was the epitome of evil.

Now she was back at Huey's and sitting in the window seat of her bedroom, staring out over the night sky. The quiet times were always the most difficult for Emma. She used to love having time alone, a few hours to read or journal, or simply do nothing, but ever since Daniel died, she couldn't tolerate downtime. Every second required something to occupy her mind to keep her from dwelling on the pain of losing him. Now the quiet of this bedroom stirred anxiety in her, and, combined with the traumatic events of the day, it threatened to drag her into a downward spiral of grief. She forced herself to shake off her sorrow and crossed the room to retrieve her laptop from her bag. She wouldn't give in to her mourning. Not yet. There would be time for that later.

She sat on the edge of her bed, opened a browser and typed Banks's name into the search box. Other than the same property tax information that Rachel had found, there wasn't anything else on the man. No social media accounts, nothing. Banks had gone to a lot of trouble to stay off the grid.

Frustration kicked in, and then a spurt of determination. Emma reached for her phone and punched in a familiar number. It rang a half dozen times before her friend finally answered. "Hey, Chloe, it's me, Emma."

"Emma! I didn't recognize this one and almost let this go to voicemail. I've been thinking about you ever since I got the photos of your brother's notebook. What's going on there?"

A dull ache of homesickness crept over Emma. She'd met Chloe the first day she joined the team, and they'd hit it off right away. She missed her and all her coworkers, and her apartment, the comfort of her own bed and the familiarity of her day-to-day routine. "I'm looking into a cold case my brother started working on before he died. I think his investigation might be why he was killed. I don't have time to go into it all now, but I need you to check on a name for me."

"Sure thing."

"Arlo Banks."

"Unusual name. Anything else you can tell me about him?"

He's evil and will haunt my nightmares forever. "He possibly worked as a horse trainer at one point, but I haven't been able to verify that." Emma gave her the address of the old farmhouse where she'd been held captive. "That's all I have. I can't find any information on him."

"Huh. Could be a fake name, but I'll see what I can do. When are you coming back to DC?"

Emma hesitated. She had no idea when it would ever be safe enough for her to return home. "Uh…well…"

"You are coming back, right?"

"Yes. Of course. There's just a lot going on here, that's all."

Chloe's voice softened. "I'm so sorry. I can't imagine." She let out a long sigh. "Take your time and don't worry about anything here. I'll call you as soon as I find something on our mystery man."

Emma hung up, glad that she'd gotten ahold of Chloe. She'd given her new number to her parents and her boss already, and to a couple of other people, but she should probably send out a text to her whole contact group. She started typing, then stopped, remembering a fleeting thought she'd had before the SUV rammed them off the road.

Daniel's notebook. She thumbed to her camera and scrolled through the photos she'd taken of his notebook. Buried in the middle of the pages were notes he'd scribbled at the scene of an accident. He'd listed three witnesses and their phone numbers. She had called them earlier without success. At the time, she'd been disappointed, but now… Her experience was that people kept their same cell numbers forever. Her parents, Chloe, Daniel… Daniel… She looked back at the numbers. Of course. How had she missed his clue?

She hurried across the hall to Logan's room.

Logan pulled on a T-shirt and answered his door. "Emma? Are you okay? Do you need help?"

"No. I'm fine." She lowered her voice. "Can I come in?"

He opened the door wider, studying her as she passed by. She wore a loose sweatshirt and baggy sweatpants, her hair piled high and messy on top of her head, without a trace of makeup on her bruised face, yet she looked amazing to him.

She held up her phone, her eyes shining brightly. "I know what Daniel wanted me to find. I can't believe I missed it. I should have known. All that time as kids that we spent exploring the woods, hunting for treasure, and I didn't catch the clue he'd left me…"

"Hold on. I have no idea what you're talking about. What clue?"

She handed him the phone and bent her head toward his as they both studied the screen. "Check out the notes he took on this vehicle accident. He's listed three witness phone numbers, but the prefixes on two don't make sense. I tried calling the numbers, but two didn't work and the third was a wrong number." She pinched and opened her fingers over the screen, enlarging the numbers. "But that's because they're not phone numbers."

He reworked the numbers in his mind. "They're not phone numbers? I don't understand."

"No, most people wouldn't. But I do because Daniel and I spent a lot of time as teens geocaching. We used coordinates all the time. I'm not sure how it all fits together yet, but I'm sure I'm right. It's so like Daniel to make up this whole report to give me GPS coordinates."

"Maybe you're right. Let's try to decipher this." He found a sheet of scratch paper in the room's desk and copied the phone numbers in Daniel's notes on the accident. The three phone numbers combined created a string of thirty digits. Separating it in the middle created what could be two geocaching coordinates. All that was missing was knowing the direction: north, south, east or west. Emma quickly pointed out that the last name for the first phone number started with *N*, the second with *A* and the third with *W*. Using just the first and last initials for the first and second set of coordinates gave them two distinct possibilities.

Together they plugged each into a geocache app on her cell phone. One showed a location in the middle of the ocean, but the other one wasn't far from River Falls.

"Did we miss something?" he asked. "The coordinates do make sense, but the location is nowhere special."

He watched as she squinted at the map on her screen. "I

don't know. There must be something out there." Frustration showed in her features. She sat back and rubbed her eyes.

"Let's call it a night. We can look at this again in the morning with a fresh perspective."

She nodded. "I don't think I'll be able to sleep. Banks is going to haunt my dreams."

Logan looked at the bruises around Emma's eye socket. Beyond the injury, he saw something he easily recognized: PTSD. He knew a lot about that. More than he wanted to know. "When you can, you'll need to find someone to talk to about what happened to you today. You've been traumatized, and it will come back to haunt you if you don't deal with it."

"Sounds like you understand something about trauma."

He swallowed hard. He'd had counseling for his PTSD and had been doing well, or so he'd thought, until that moment in the ER...

"Logan."

His head popped up.

"Do you want to talk about it?"

The air between them seemed to shrink. "It's not easy for me to talk about." He needed to finish telling her what had really happened in the ER with Daniel. How his flashback had caused him to hesitate. How any other doctor might have been able to save Daniel. How he'd failed.

He needed to unburden himself, break the guilt that gripped his heart. But suddenly her hand covered his, and she leaned forward, waiting for his response. He appreciated that and ached to draw her close, hold her. Kiss her. He stared at her lips, knowing he should pull back, but his pulse quickened, and he closed the distance between them, pressed his lips against hers, gently at first, then more demanding. Her hands brushed against his chest and found their way to his neck, bringing him closer. Then, as their kiss deepened, he pulled back.

She let out a little sigh. "What's wrong?"

Her face was inches from his, and her gaze held so much tenderness and compassion, but how would she look at him if she knew the truth?

"There's a lot you don't know about me."

She smiled with such innocence that it hurt him. "I know that you're kind and compassionate and virtuous."

He crossed his arms. "That's just it. I'm not any of those things." Virtue didn't build a relationship on a lie. Withholding the truth wasn't kind, but selfish.

"Why would you say that? I've seen the way you are with your family and your desire to help the people in this community, and all that you've done for me."

"Emma, there's something you should—"

She stepped forward and touched his face. "No. You don't understand. I admire you. And your faith. The thing is that ever since Daniel died, I've been angry with God. I don't want to admit it, but it's true."

He backed up, a stab of hurt piercing his soul now. She dropped her hand, confusion flashing in her eyes.

I'm responsible for that, he thought. What he had done not only devastated her life but damaged her faith. He should have never been in the ER that night. He was overly tired, pushing himself to the limit for one more shift and for the overtime pay for his clinic. He knew better than to let himself become exhausted during a shift. He'd been greedy, and a good man had lost his life because of it. And he'd hurt Emma's heart and faith because of it, as well.

"Logan, what is it? What's wrong? You look sick."

He could barely bring himself to look at her. "You should go. If we're going to check out the area at daybreak, we need a good night's sleep."

TWELVE

Moonlight filtered through the mini blinds on Emma's bedroom window and cast lines across the walls. She'd been staring at them for hours while trying to sort through her emotions after the kiss shared between her and Logan. It'd felt wonderful and right, and yet he pulled away and dismissed her. Had she done something wrong? Was it because she'd admitted that she wasn't as strong in her faith as him? Was he angry with her?

She tossed and turned, and when she did finally fall asleep, she slipped into horrid nightmares, reliving her week—being shot at, the car wreck, rats, and on and on—until she woke the next morning groggy and irritable, her muscles sore and her body tense with anxiety over facing Logan again.

She showered and dressed for a day in the woods, threw on Daniel's flannel jacket and pulled her hair into a tight ponytail. Her face had gone from red and swollen to pale with dark, sickly blue bruises and a thin V-shaped line from her cheek to neck to ear. No wonder Logan didn't want to kiss her. She spent a few minutes attempting to cover them with makeup, gave up and headed down for coffee.

Logan was in the kitchen, leaning against the counter as he finished a phone call. He pocketed his phone and poured her a mug of coffee. He paused as he handed it to her, his eyes growing wide.

She tried not to think of how horrible she looked. "Don't worry—I look worse than I feel." Logan looked a bit beaten up himself; his eyes were sunken and lines etched worry deep into his forehead. Had he had trouble sleeping, too?

"I've got news," he said.

"Good or bad?"

"Both. Pruitt called a little while ago. He wanted to let me know first thing that they found Banks's abandoned vehicle at the train station in Hinton. There was only one train out of the area last night. They're working to track down where he got off. But it looks like he's gone."

Her relief was almost palpable. "You didn't say anything about the coordinates, did you? Or where we're going today?"

"No. Nothing."

"Good. We're getting close to putting all this behind us. I'm sure of it. Whatever evidence Daniel left for me at these coordinates holds the key to finishing this for good. All we've got to do is retrieve it."

Logan's grimace exaggerated his worry lines.

"What's wrong? Aren't you thrilled that Banks is gone?"

"It's not that. It's Rachel. She started bleeding last night. Joe called me this morning."

Emma gasped. "Oh, no. I'm so sorry, Logan."

"It's too early to know if she's losing the baby or not. I pray not."

"You should be with her. I can check out the coordinates alone."

"I was going to go see her, but Joe wants her to rest for now. She's talked to her doctor, and Joe and his parents are with her, so there's not a lot I can do right now. I'll check in on her later. But I was counting on Joe going with us for re-inforcement. These coordinates point to a remote area. We'd be out there alone and unprotected. I think we should wait."

"Wait? Why? You just told me that they think Banks is long gone. The threat is off. The biggest challenge now is finding the cache and the evidence that Daniel hid."

His jaw muscles twitched. "Listen, when I regained consciousness after the accident, Banks was there, pointing a gun at my head. He would have shot me if that trucker hadn't come along when he did. And the way he shot up the restaurant, not caring who he hit... This isn't a man who just gives up. We know he's after you, and we can't underestimate him. He means to get what he's after, no matter the cost."

Emma cringed. Why didn't he tell her before that Banks nearly shot him? Did she have the right to ask him to put his life at risk again? She thought of Rachel and the danger she'd brought to Logan and his whole family. Worse, the stress of all this could have been what brought on the threat of a miscarriage for Rachel. She had no right to hurt this family anymore.

Logan continued, "And when I think of how he terrorized you in that cellar... He was going to kill you. Is all this worth losing your life over? I can't imagine Daniel would want that."

"Are you asking me to quit? And what about Kate? I thought we were both on a quest to find our answers. Are you giving up on finding out what happened to your sister?"

"No. I want to find the truth as much as you do. But I don't want to be reckless about it. There's a bigger picture here that we're not seeing. We don't know what motivated Banks, who he's tied in with or who else is involved. We don't even know who was driving the gray sports car.

Maybe Banks, he's obviously doing someone's dirty work, but we can't be sure."

"But Banks is gone for now." She couldn't quit, not when they were this close. "No one knows that we have the coordinates. I think it's safe enough to go. Don't worry—I'll be careful."

She reached for her gear bag next to the kitchen door, filled a water bottle and threw it in, then rummaged through the cabinet for a couple of portable snacks. The kitchen felt small, although it was just the two of them.

"Emma, you can't go alone."

"Well, I can't stay here forever."

He smiled. "You're going to go no matter what I say, aren't you?"

"If you're right, and whoever is behind this is still after me, I won't be completely safe until I learn what Daniel wanted me to find. The quickest way to end this is to expose the truth. If I wait, I run the risk of being killed before I can uncover the evidence. Banks is gone, so it's a perfect opportunity to finish this now."

With his arms folded, his attention solely on her, he leaned back against the counter. She stood paralyzed in a haze of uncertainty, while his gaze penetrated hers. What did he see in her eyes? Did he sense her feelings? Could he see through her brave front to the fear that filled her heart? More than anything, she wanted to take two tiny steps forward and press herself into his arms, where she'd feel safe and protected.

He straightened and took a step forward, nodding in resignation. "Okay, I'll get my stuff."

He turned to grab his own supplies, and she blurted, "Why would you risk your life for me? Because you need your own answers about Kate?"

His shoulders slumped. "Yes. That's part of it."

"But there's more to it, isn't there? Something that you wanted to tell me last night."

He turned. "Yes, there's a lot more to it. And I'll tell you soon, but now's not the time. We need to stay focused."

Huey's Range Rover had been a total loss. Luckily, insurance would cover the cost to replace the vehicle, and Huey was good-natured about the whole ordeal. "I can replace a vehicle, but not a friend," he'd said. He even offered to loan them another one of his vehicles today—his Mustang GT. Logan had ridden in that Mustang, pined over its sleek, race red exterior and creamy black leather seats, and dreamed of owning a car just like it. The opportunity to drive it today was tempting, but he passed on Huey's gracious offer and was back in his truck again, heading toward the coordinates destination.

On the way, they passed by the spot where Daniel was killed. The spot had been shown on the news and was marked by a blue cross. He glanced across the seat and saw Emma staring out the window, almost folded in on herself, her brother's flannel jacket practically swallowing her small frame. She'd worn it ever since Deputy Davis gave it to her.

He reached for her hand to comfort her and felt relieved when she didn't pull back. He held it until he needed both hands on the wheel to pull into the trailhead. He parked and studied the GPS again, making a slight adjustment to their direction. "Looks like it's about a two-mile hike to the coordinates. Hopefully we can get in, get it and get back within a couple of hours." She nodded, and they got out of the vehicle.

On the trail, he struggled to keep up with Emma's pace. Even at this elevation and moving up the mountain, she was a strong hiker. "For a city girl, you can handle yourself on the mountain."

She laughed, and it filled him with joy. He liked the way she smiled and laughed and so many other things about her. He decided to take a chance and bring up something that had been on his mind. "If we happened to live in the same area, would you consider…?" He kept his tone cool and steady, but inside he was shaking. "I mean, would you ever go out with me?"

"Only if it doesn't involve being tied up, beaten, shot at or chased down by big cars."

"I was thinking more along the lines of a movie and dinner."

"That would be a definite 'yes,' then. When will you be in DC?" She turned around and smiled.

"DC? I didn't mean… I guess I wondered if you'd…" Her smile faded.

"It's just that it's hard for me to get away. Night shifts in the ER, my clinic during the day."

"I understand, but when this is over, I'll be going back to DC. It's my home. My work is there and my friends."

"But you're a writer. Can't you do that from anywhere?" She stopped hiking, and he saw her lips press together.

"I'm an investigative journalist. Do you know how competitive that is?"

She turned back and walked faster now, talking over her shoulder. He rechecked his GPS to make sure they were still on route and then doubled his speed to catch up with her.

She cast him a sideways glance. "It's taken a lot of work to get where I am. My byline is getting noticed, and newspapers seek me out for stories now. DC is where a lot of news breaks, political and otherwise. It'd be career suicide to leave there now."

"I'm sorry. I didn't mean to downplay your work. I didn't know your location was so important to your career. I mean, stories are everywhere."

"Not the stories I want to write."

"Oh, I see." A quiver ran through his gut. He thought that God had sent him someone who... He swallowed back his disappointment, accepting the reality. What did he expect? Once she knew what happened in the ER that night, she would never talk to him again anyway. *Why does it have to be like this?* And why did he feel so strongly about her? No matter how he felt about her, it was clear they had met for a reason. He couldn't guess God's plan. But to both be free to go their separate ways and live their lives as God wanted, they would first need to discover the truth about Daniel and, he hoped, about Kate.

She pushed a branch out of the way, ducked around it and held it for him. Their gazes met as he passed, his heartbeat kicking up a notch as he took the lead, pausing here and there to check their progress. Cell service was spotty now, so he switched to a paper map where he'd marked off their route to the coordinates. "Looks like it's just over this ridge." He stripped off his windbreaker and stuffed it into his pack. The cool breeze hit his sweat-soaked T-shirt. He shivered and scanned the woods.

"Do you see something?"

"No. I'm just paranoid. This almost seems too easy." The breeze whistled around tree trunks, rustling leaves. Squirrels chatted, and somewhere far off a crow croaked out a series of caws. "Let's just get the cache and get out of here," he said.

Emma trudged through the underbrush, her thighs burning as she crested the ridge and looked down on the ravine below. The slanted rooflines of several crumbled brick buildings poked through the tree canopy, and a long conveyor system snaked through the trees, its rusted trusses overrun by weeds.

"It's an abandoned mining camp," Emma said as soon as Logan caught up to her. "I've been here before. Daniel and I came here when we were teenagers. We were always hiking and exploring, and somehow one day we ended up here." She surveyed the area. "We didn't come in from this direction, though." She pointed across the gorge. "We hiked through the valley over there."

"I never knew this was out here. It's like a piece of history." Logan's gaze swept over the area. "Over there must be what remains of the fan house. It would have been used to circulate air through the mine. And there, that would have been the powder house where explosives were stored, and... Oh, man, I wish my dad was here. He would have loved seeing this." He shaded his eyes and pointed to a dilapidated structure. "Look at that. See all that timber? I bet that's what's left of the head house, and that's—"

"We need to figure out how to get in there." Emma pointed to the main adit, a cave-like entrance on the side of the rocky hill. It was blocked by a tall chain-link fence.

Logan frowned. "You want to go into the mine? No, not a good idea, and I don't think Daniel would have put evidence in there anyway. How would he get in there? It's got that fence and... Well, it's too dangerous. It makes more sense that he put it in one of these outbuildings."

"Yeah, the fence is new. It wasn't there when we were kids." She shrugged. "I don't know how he got in, but he would have known that I'd look there first. We explored in there when we were here. I remember that day like it was yesterday. Daniel was against going into the mine, but I begged and begged until I wore him down. I was so curious and headstrong back then."

"Good to know you outgrew that."

She laughed, then grew serious again. "Looking back on it, it was one of the more foolish things we did. We could have been hurt or worse. We never told Mom and Dad what we'd done." She smiled. "We kept a lot of secrets from them."

She started down into the gorge without him. "Wait here and keep a lookout. I'll go in and get it. I know where he would have left it, and it's not far inside the entrance."

The trek through the gorge was rough, with overgrown scrub and uneven ground. She had to maneuver the weeds and long-ago discarded debris before even reaching the steep slope leading up to the mine's entrance. Logan trudged behind her, but she didn't stop to wait for him. She reached the fence, ignored the warnings and no trespassing signs, and searched until she found an opening just big enough to slide through. She then squeezed between the haphazard boards that had been fastened across the cave-like entrance and blinked against the darkness, fumbling with her phone light.

Logan slipped in behind her.

"Didn't want me to have all the fun?" she asked.

He unclipped a small flashlight from his belt and aimed the beam around the opening. "Something like that."

He kept the light forward as they made their way deeper into the mine. Sharp-edged stone walls, black with coal dust, led them farther. They stepped gingerly to avoid the rusted rails along the floor used for carts that had brought the buried storehouse of coal to the long-gone mining company.

"It's like descending into the bowels of the earth," Emma

said. The musty, earthy air took her breath away. She folded her arms and tucked her chin into the collar of Daniel's jacket. It must have been ten degrees cooler inside the mine.

"Do you know where we're going?" Logan's voice echoed softly.

"Up ahead, there's a spot where we carved our initials. He would have put it there." Her senses felt stunted, deprived, and Logan's flashlight shone like little more than a small prick of hope inside a dark cavern of questions. And despite the cold, she was sweating. A slick film instantly clung to her skin. A rodent scurried through the flashlight beam, and Emma startled and shrieked, her cry echoing through the cavern as she stumbled and pitched forward.

Logan caught her. "You okay?"

She straightened and sucked in a deep breath that tasted like sulfur. "Rat. That was a rat."

"It's gone, okay? It's more scared of you than you are of it."

"I doubt that." She thought she could do this, but the darkness, the stone walls, the rats—it was taking her right back to the cellar.

"You can do this, Emma." Logan held on to her hand, focusing the beam more at their feet as they started their descent again. They moved slowly, stopping every few feet to shine the light on the walls. Finally, the light hit on a pair of crudely scratched initials: EH, DH.

She traced her fingers over each letter, remembering how Daniel had used his new Swiss Army knife to carve the initials and his disappointment when the blade snapped against the hardness of the stone wall. She stretched forward and reached above the initials to feel along a narrow ledge formed by striations in the rock, then jerked back. What if…? Could rats climb that high?

"Hold this," Logan said, handing her the flashlight. "I'll search."

"No, that's okay. I can do this." She reached up and felt along the ledge until her fingers bumped against something hard. Not a rat, but something made of metal. "I've got it!" Her voice echoed back at her. "I was right. Here it is." She showed Logan a small metal box not much bigger than her palm.

Logan moved closer, focusing the light over her shoulder.

Emma's hands shook as she opened the container and emptied the contents into her hand. "A flash drive." Her heart sank. If only it was something else, maybe a name, or a photograph that would provide an immediate answer. Instead, they would have to wait until they could access the information on the device. She slipped it into her pocket and felt along the ledge for anything else.

"Is that it?" Logan asked.

"Guess so. Let's head back to Huey's and see what's on it."

They turned back, orienting themselves toward the streaks of daylight shining through the missing boards at the cave's entrance.

"It'd be quicker to stop by the clinic to use the computer than to head all the way back to Huey's," Logan said. "Do you want to—" A shadow crossed over the entrance, blocking the sunlight.

Emma jumped back and clenched Logan's arm. "Did you see that? What was it?"

"Shh." Logan flicked off his flashlight.

They stood in the darkness, straining their gazes toward the entrance. The shadow morphed into a human figure, and a flashlight flipped on. A beam of light swept across the cave.

"We've been followed," Logan hissed into her ear, and the beam was suddenly on them.

He yanked her back just as a gunshot rang out. Emma cringed and clasped her ears. The shot sounded like thunder inside the cave. The next shot ricocheted off the rock in front of them. Another shot hit nearby, and another, like pinballs bouncing in a machine, as Logan pulled her deeper into the cave. She moved with her hands in front of her, paddling against the darkness, feeling for obstacles. Several times she stumbled on the pitted cave floor, falling forward, scraping her palms against the rough rocks until they reached the bottom of the shaft where it forked in several directions. She started to the left, and they moved as quickly as they could on the uneven ground, her breath ragged and her heart pounding in her ears. Then they slowed their pace and stopped to listen.

"I don't hear anything," Logan whispered. "He must have gone the other way."

Emma pulled her cell from her pocket, her finger sliding over the screen until she found the flashlight app again. Logan swept his own flashlight beam, and Emma her cell light, over the mole-like tunnel.

Logan's voice wavered when he spoke. "We're not in the main mine anymore."

Emma's nerves felt raw under her skin. *This is bad. Really bad.*

The shaft had changed. No longer uniform and machine dug, it appeared to be hand hewed. The walls were narrow, and the ceiling overhead was nothing more than layers of sheetlike rocks propped up and supported by crudely cut logs.

"This can't be safe." She looked around. "We can't go this way. Let's go back."

"No. He'll be waiting outside the entrance for us. We need to find another exit."

Emma took a couple of deep breaths and fought to tamp down the panic roaring inside her. *Think. Think.*

Logan tugged at her arm. "Let's go."

"No, not yet," Emma said. She flipped off her cell light. "The more we move, the easier it'll be for him to find us. Let's go stealth. Wait it out and hope that he took a different tunnel. He'll eventually assume we got out and give up." The thought terrified her, but she knew it was the smartest thing to do.

Logan agreed. He pulled her close and turned off his own flashlight. The darkness swallowed them whole and confounded her senses as if they'd been thrust into a black hole, with no orientation of up or down, left or right. The air was void of movement, with only the faint sound of dripping water coming from somewhere far away. Again, she remembered the cellar and the rats, and fear threatened her every sense. Her chin trembled. "I'm going to turn my cell light back on. Just for a few seconds. I can't—"

He wrapped both arms around her, pulling her deeper into his body, and the fear in her quieted. She closed her eyes and forced her thoughts to focus on a childhood memory, her and Daniel playing outside in the woods next to their house, the bright sky, the smell of pine, sounds of birds, Daniel's laughter. Then her thoughts betrayed her as she mentally stumbled into a poignant memory, something she'd whispered to him that day: *We'll always be together, Danny, you and me, forever.* Her breath caught, and she opened her eyes. *Now's not the time to do this. Stay focused, Emma.*

"Did you get a look at him?" she whispered. "Do you think it was Banks?"

"I didn't see a face. Wouldn't know if it was Banks or not anyway."

"It must be Banks." She shifted and felt her pocket. "He was after the flash drive that day in the cellar. He kept asking me where it was hidden. This must be what he wanted all along."

Logan said, "Probably. And he thought you knew where it was this whole time. That's why he's worked so hard to keep you alive."

"Keep me alive? But he ran us off the road. He tried to kill both of us."

"Did he? Another mile or so and we would have been in the mountains. If he'd forced us off the road there, we would have gone over a cliff to our deaths. Instead, he pushed us off the road while we were still in the flats."

"Which was dangerous enough."

"I'm not saying it wasn't a risk from his point of view. There was a chance that both of us would have been killed, but he was out of options. And he didn't care if you were hurt. He only needed you alive enough to tell him where the evidence was hidden."

"But he's tried to kill me several times."

"Not you. Me. That's why he took you from the accident scene—he was intent on killing me. He wanted me out of the way. Which makes me think that when Crawford was shot, the other bullet was meant for me, not you. Otherwise, at the accident, why wouldn't he have killed you when he had the chance?"

She shuddered. "Maybe, but he wasn't trying to keep me alive out there in the woods by Daniel's cabin or at the restaurant. He was shooting to kill."

"It's been about the flash drive all along. He might have

thought that you found it at the cabin and all he had to do was kill you and take it from you."

She knew he was right, but… "Then the drive-by shooting at the restaurant doesn't fit."

"No, it doesn't. There's no way he could abduct you in that situation, and killing us wouldn't get him any closer to the flash drive."

A couple of beats of silence passed as she stared into the darkness. "There's something else. Pruitt kept asking me if I was holding something back. Do you think he knew about the flash drive?"

"I have no idea. I can't figure out his part in all this."

"But even if Pruitt is involved, how did he know to follow us out here? You didn't tell him our plans, did you?"

"No. But when Pruitt responded to the accident scene, he could have traced Huey's vehicle and found his residence. If that's the case, it was just a matter of watching Huey's and waiting for us to make a move. Or have Banks watch and wait for us."

Could be, she thought, but… "How would anyone follow us through the woods without us knowing? We would have heard their movement. No one is that stealthy."

"True. It's not adding up, is it?"

"No. But it will as soon as I see what's on this—" Scuffing footprints echoed from the shaft.

Logan released her and started to stand. "We've got to move," he whispered.

It was too late. A light danced around the walls and landed on them, shining directly into Emma's eyes, paralyzing her until Logan yanked her to her feet. "Run!" She jolted forward, lost her balance and plummeted toward the ground, her hands skidding on rough rock and fingertips sinking into the sludge.

Crack! The sound of the shot reverberated in the narrow cavern, followed by a low rumble that sounded like distant thunder.

Emma shrieked and covered her head while small, rocky debris pummeled her body.

THIRTEEN

"Emma?" Logan whispered. The air was grave-like still. Dust stung his nostrils and mixed with his sweat, sticking to him like a second skin. He coughed and wiped his eyes with one hand, then found her with the other. "Emma. Are you okay?"

"Yes." She peeled away from him and kept her voice low. "Where is he?"

"I don't know. I dropped my flashlight." Logan crouched and ran his hands over the uneven floor, his gaze catching on a slight glow ten feet away. He maneuvered over fallen rock until he reached it. Digging through debris, he finally pulled free the assailant's heavy steel flashlight. He aimed the beam, relief washing over him as it illuminated Emma. She seemed okay, but his relief turned to dread when he saw a foot protruding from under a pile of rock.

"He's buried. Help me get these off him." He propped the flashlight nearby and hurried to free the man from the rubble. Emma joined him, scooping up the flashlight and pointing it directly where Logan was working. He lifted the last of the debris off the man and brushed dust off his face.

"It's Banks," Emma said.

Logan turned his attention to checking for a pulse and broken bones. "He's badly injured, but alive. Likely internal injuries, as well. We need to go for help, or he won't make it." He picked up the flashlight. "Come on. Let's get out of here."

He took her hand and together they wound through the maze of shafts until they reached the mine's entrance. They emerged covered in a thin layer of black dust. He blinked against the bright sunlight and looked her over. No blood or obvious injuries, but he paused on her face. Despite the dirt that clung to her cheeks and hair, he thought she was the most beautiful woman he'd ever seen.

"Are you hurt anywhere?" he asked.

"I'm fine, but you're bleeding." She reached up and ran her fingertips over his jaw, tilting his head to the side. "Here, on your temple."

"I'm okay." He took her hand and turned it over. Her palms were red and puffy where angry scratches were still fresh. "This must hurt," he said, and unable to resist the temptation, he pressed his lips to her injured skin.

She exhaled, close enough that he felt her breath whisper across his face. He ran his fingers along her arm, neck, and cupped her chin, tipping her head up to his. Her eyes closed, and her lips parted slightly. Every nerve in him cried for a taste of her kiss, but he pulled back. He'd already crossed that line and felt how wrong it was. Soon, he thought, but not until he could build their relationship on an honest foundation.

She opened her eyes. "What is it?"

He smiled at her and rubbed a smear of coal dust from her cheek. "I'll explain soon. I promise. Let's get going."

They were almost to the trailhead before he could get enough cell service to get a 911 call out. As soon as he finished relaying the information to the dispatcher, Emma held out her hands. "Give me your truck keys."

"What? Why?"

"You have to stay here and lead the paramedics to Banks. He needs help right away, and there's no way they'll find him without you."

He didn't like how this sounded. "We'll stay and wait for them together."

"Listen, once Pruitt finds out what happened here, there will be a lot of explaining to do. Eventually he'll want to know exactly why we came up here, and I won't be able to keep the flash drive a secret. I'll have to turn it over to him before I can read the information, and I'll never figure out Daniel's secret. All this work we've done will be for nothing."

"I understand. And you're right. I just don't want you out there alone."

"I'll be okay. I'll drive straight to Huey's, no stops. Once I get there, I'll copy everything for safekeeping." She pushed her hand closer. "Please, Logan. The keys. We've gotten this far, and I don't want to lose everything Daniel sacrificed his life for."

Logan fished the keys out of his jacket pocket and placed them in her palm. "I'll call Huey and let him know you're coming. He'll be watching for you." He reached out and grasped her face between his hands and lowered his chin until she met his gaze. "You'll go straight there. No stops?"

"No stops. Promise."

He leaned in and touched his lips to her forehead. "Be safe. Please."

He watched her leave, his heart heavy with worry. Was he doing the right thing, waiting and not going with her? Banks might be out of the picture, half dead or worse if they couldn't get him to medical care soon, but how many others were involved? Pruitt? If so, she was safer not being with the police. But would she be okay out there on her own? Something she'd mentioned earlier nagged at the back of his mind: How *did* Banks know where to find them?

The sun had set by the time Emma pulled into the alley and parked behind Huey's place. She'd checked her rear-view mirror a thousand times on the way here. There were no signs that she had been followed. Still, she couldn't shake the feeling that someone was watching her.

She turned off the engine and stared at the backyard. The security light didn't reach far enough, and shadows loomed around the cluster of bushes near the fence gate. Anyone could be hiding... *Stop! This is silly.* She'd been careful. No one had followed her—she was sure of it.

She needed to get inside and access the flash drive but took a moment and asked God for the courage to see this through. Peace settled over her, and she breathed deeply, stepped out of the truck and double-checked her pocket. The flash drive was still there.

She glanced up and down the alley before starting for the backyard gate, walking purposefully and confidently, until the clattering of a metal garbage can stopped her in her tracks. The neighbor's dog broke into a series of rapid, high-pitched barks, and then another dog joined in, and another, their barks set off in succession like a round in an orchestrated chorus.

She froze in a stupor of fear and indecisiveness. *Run for the house door or back to the car?* She chided herself, her inner voice telling her, *Think clearly, stay focused, don't be such a wimp...* "Emma. Over here!"

Her head snapped to the right of the house and a small side door. Huey briefly emerged from the shadows and waved her forward. She let out a sigh of relief and hurried over to him.

Inside they climbed a small, rickety flight of wood stairs to the third-floor attic. "These stairs were used for servants," he told her. "So they could move through the house unseen."

"I had no idea these were here."

"We hardly use them. They're too narrow for most of us older guys to navigate. But I thought it'd be better to bring you in quietly and let you get right to work. Logan filled me in a little. And he asked me to keep an eye out for you."

She smiled at the idea of Logan rallying his friend to help keep her safe.

Huey glanced over his shoulder and noticed her expression. "Logan's a good guy. He'll make someone a good husband one day."

She had no idea how to respond and was glad they'd reached the top floor. Apache greeted them as they exited onto the landing. Emma had seen the narrow door earlier, but assumed it went to a storage closet, not a hidden set of stairs.

Huey scooped up and cradled the cat as he showed her into her room, where a tray with a sandwich, brownie and a carafe of coffee waited. "Thank you," she said. "I'm starved and badly in need of caffeine."

"Thought you might be. I'll let you get to work."

Emma thanked him again, and as soon as he left, she pulled out her laptop and set it on the small desk. Her coal-dust fingerprints smudged the laptop's case. She started to wipe her hands on her leggings, only to realize she looked like a chimney sweep from head to foot, ready to contaminate anything she touched. No matter—she had to check out the flash drive.

She switched on the lamp, opened her laptop and inserted it. Several files popped onto her screen.

Her heart raced as she clicked on the first file, titled Murray, J.-Homicide. It was the original case file from ten years ago. She skimmed through the reports and witness testimonies and shuffled through the crime scene photos, but found nothing more than what she already knew. She'd look more closely at it later.

The next file was a recently signed affidavit from the convenience store owner, Jay Turner, stating that he had identified Crawford and Mink as the two individuals who had robbed the convenience store the night of Jack Murray's murder. He verified that he'd handed store surveillance videos over to the police as evidence of the robbery. There was also a signed affidavit from Crawford, in exchange for leniency for a possession charge. It confirmed everything Mink had told Emma about that night, including the name of the girl that they'd picked up and partied with—Mary J. Flann. Emma jotted down the name, planning to look the woman up on the internet. There was no affidavit from Mary, but hopefully the convenience store owner's testimony and Crawford's written testimony would be enough to clear Mink of murder and get him out of prison.

The third file was titled Murray Farms and contained a list of auctions where Seth had sold or acquired his horses. Most of them were taken from horse auction publications. There were three years of auctions listed. Seth frequented the same auctions over and over. Nothing unusual about that, she thought. Also attached was a photo from what looked to be a horse auction. It showed a horse in the center of an arena, an announcer on a high podium and bleachers full of spectators. Emma searched the photo for its meaning, but it was lost on her. She didn't recognize the location, or the horse being sold, and the image was too small to distinguish the faces in the crowd. *What were you trying to tell me with this info? What am I missing?*

She sat back and tried to imagine Daniel's thought process. In his message he'd said that he planned to explain the entire case to her in person when they met. He'd assumed that he would be alive to fill her in on the rest of the details.

Only he wasn't.

Oh, Daniel. She blinked back the tears threatening her eyes and closed the horse auction file. She'd look at this again later. She moved the tray of food near to her desk and poured a large cup of coffee but stopped before touching the sandwich and stared at her blackened hands. Shuddering at the thought of ingesting who knew what types of toxins from the mine, she stripped off her clothes and jumped in the shower for a quick cleanup, watching the gray water swirl down the drain. Moments later, hair wet and dressed in a clean sweatshirt and leggings, she finally took a bite of the sandwich as she checked her phone for any missed messages, hoping for a call from Logan, letting her know that he was on his way back. Nothing.

Two more files. One titled Mary J. Flann and the other labeled County Record. She sighed and clicked on the second-to-last file, hoping for something more substantial than what she'd found so far.

It contained a scan of a high school yearbook picture for Mary J. Flann. She was a pretty girl, even though she appeared to be plagued by the usual teenage acne. Emma had had her fair share of blemishes in her teens, plus braces and thick glasses. High school was no cakewalk, that was for sure.

She leaned closer to the screen and studied the face under the short mop of dark hair. There was something familiar in the girl's gaze, or maybe it was how she tilted her chin and stared defiantly at the camera.

Emma's skin prickled as she continued reading. The next file was from the county register's office, a divorce decree, between Mary J. Flann and Robert Davis. It tapped into what was already niggling in the back of her mind. She re-opened the high school photo and looked closely. Add years to her age and change the hair color and... *Davis. Deputy Davis.* Mary J. Flann was Jess Davis.

She was the girl Crawford and Mink were out with that night? Why hadn't she come forward earlier? And now she was a cop, certainly she would say... Unless... Cold dread slithered through Emma's core.

She stood and crossed the room, patting down Daniel's jacket where it hung by the door. *Where is it? Where...?* Finally her fingers brushed against something sewn into the fabric under the collar. She dropped the jacket onto the floor and stood back, her mind racing. Was it possible that the whole time she'd been wearing her brother's jacket...? She rifled through the desk drawer, found a pair of scissors, knelt and thrust the blade into the fabric, frantically digging and tearing at the cloth until she revealed a thin black square tracking device.

It had been there the whole time. Jess had been shadowing her. She was the traitor inside the police department. She told Banks where to find them. *What now?* Call Pruitt? Flush the tracking device? What should she do? Jess, or some other evil person, could be closing in on her at this very moment.

Her phone buzzed. She startled, then relaxed when she saw that it was Chloe. "Hey, Chloe. I'll have to call you back. I've got a problem here and—"

"No. This can't wait." Chloe's voice was high-pitched

and thin. "Emma. It's taken me a while, but I found some information for you, and it's not good news. Looks like the property where you were held was purchased by Arlo Banks a little over ten years ago, but a deeper dive into his name showed he had an expunged record."

Emma moved back to her desk and began downloading the files from the flash drive directly to her computer. She addressed an email to Chloe and attached the files.

"Were you able to access it?"

"Yes. He served seven years in the Texas State Pen for drug trafficking."

Emma stopped typing. "Drug trafficking?"

"Looks that way."

Emma took a second to digest the information. What had Daniel stumbled into? "Hold on a sec," she told Chloe. She called up the file from the auctions. The manifesto Daniel had included showed sales at major auctions across the US. Were drugs being transported with the horses, in horse trailers or in special feed bins? And somehow it seemed Jess Davis was connected, but how? And how did Jack Murray's murder and Kate's disappearance fit into all this?

"Emma? Are you still there?"

Emma blinked. "Yeah. I'm here. Listen, I'm sending you an email with the files that Daniel left for me. I'm not quite sure what all this means yet. I need more time to look into it all. Watch for my email." She told her about Deputy Davis and the tracking device. "She's been following me. As soon as I get these files to you, I'm packing up and moving from this location. I'm not sure how deep the corruption goes, but if anything happens to me, make sure this information goes to—"

Someone yelled; a door slammed; scuffling sounds came from the hallway outside her room. Emma put down her phone and reached for the scissors on the desk. She gripped them like a dagger and moved cautiously toward the door. Suddenly it crashed open, the smoke alarm in the hallway blared, and Huey burst into the room, shouting, "Fire! Fire! Get out."

FOURTEEN

Rescue efforts were underway as deputies hauled lights and equipment up the mountain and into the mine like ants ascending an anthill. Logan had just returned to the trailhead to help with the medical supplies when Pruitt arrived. He spoke briefly with his deputies before making a beeline for Logan.

"I want some answers," Pruitt said. "How did you and Banks end up in that mine? What were you doing in there?"

Logan hesitated. Emma had left only forty-five minutes ago. Had it been enough time for her to get to Huey's and look at the flash drive?

Pruitt sighed impatiently. "I sense mistrust, Greer. What's the problem? We've known each other a long time."

"Yes, I remember. We met for the first time when you showed up on my doorstep asking about my sister's whereabouts in connection to Jack Murray's murder."

"Doing my job, that's all." Beads of sweat broke along Pruitt's upper lip. "Just like I'm trying to do now. Banks is half dead up there in that mine, and I want to know why. Did you follow him out here?"

"No…"

"Then he followed you." Pruitt frowned. "Why were you out here in the first place?"

Logan looked at the ground and shuffled his feet.

Pruitt scoffed and surveyed the parking lot, his eyes scanning every car. "Did you borrow another car to get up here today or did you drive your truck?"

"My truck."

"Where is it?" Pruitt swiped his hand over his head and wiped it on his trousers. "You weren't up here alone with Banks, were you? The Hayes woman was with you. Where's she now?"

"We came here to look for something her brother hid in the mine."

"And what was that?"

"Daniel Hayes didn't die in a highway homicide. He died because he was investigating a cold case. But I feel certain you knew that already."

"I don't like what you're implying." Pruitt's features hardened. "I think about that kid every day. He was one of us. Family. And I knew he was working the Murray homicide. I gave him permission. As far as I know, he didn't come up with any new leads."

"You're wrong about that."

"What are you saying?"

"He left behind a flash drive with evidence that implicates Jack Murray's murderer. That's what Banks has been after this whole time. That's what we found in the mine. Daniel hid it there."

"Are you saying that the Hayes woman found evidence in a homicide investigation? And she fled the area with it?"

"She doesn't know who to trust."

Pruitt's jaw clenched, and Logan half expected the sheriff would whip out a set of handcuffs and arrest him on the spot, but the buzz of the man's cell phone interrupted. Pruitt slipped it from his pocket and looked at the display, answering immediately. "Pruitt here…What? Where?… Okay, I'm on my way."

He turned and yelled out to one of the deputies. "Blaze in the historic district, on Monroe and Fayette. Dispatch says there's several elderly residents. Fire is responding to another call, so we've got a unit coming in from Hinton, but it's about twenty minutes out still. I'm heading into town." He thumbed toward Logan. "Bring this guy into my office. I'll need to question him later."

Logan reached out to stop Pruitt. "Wait. I've got to go with you."

The sheriff batted away Logan's hand, his voice hard. "Go with the deputy to—"

"No! You don't understand. That address is where we've been staying. Emma's there right now."

"Emma? What is it?" Chloe's panicked voice came over the cell on the floor.

Emma dropped the scissors and snatched up the phone. "Fire. The house is on fire. I've sent an email with the information from the flash drive."

"Just get out of there, Emma. Now!"

"Come on, Emma!" Huey called over his shoulder as he ran to alert others.

Emma pocketed her phone and the flash drive, threw her laptop and cell into her bag, slung it over her shoulder and slipped into the hallway. Smoke billowed through the cracks around the small door that led to the back stairs. She threw open Logan's door—empty. She double-checked his bathroom. Empty. Coughing, she headed back into the hall and for the main staircase, running into Huey as he led a confused resident to safety.

"Second floor's clear," he yelled over the alarm. Its sound throbbed in her head.

"Upstairs is clear, too."

She helped Huey get the resident out the front door and to the rest of the group huddled on the yard. Sirens shrieked in the distance. Huey looked over the group, counting heads under his breath. "Everyone's out. Thank God. And they all look okay."

Shaken, but safe, Emma thought. Everyone stood in shock as they watched flames leap from the roof of the at-tached garage.

"It hasn't reached the house yet," someone said. "Let's get the hose. Maybe we can put it out."

"We should wait for the fire department," someone else said.

An argument broke out while Emma scanned the crowd, dread growing in the pit of her stomach. "Apache. Did any-one grab Apache?"

Huey turned back to the house, his face horror-struck.

"I'm going back for him."

"Emma, no! It's too dangerous."

She ignored him and ran toward the house.

Inside, acrid smoke darkened the air, burning her nose and throat and coating her tongue with a gummy chemical taste. Her eyes dripped tears. She coughed and pulled her shirt over her nose and mouth as she groped her way along the wall. On the other side, flames cracked and popped as fire consumed the garage. She pushed away fleeting thoughts of gasoline and paint and a thousand explosive items stored in most garages and kept moving. She only had one shot to find the cat; there wasn't time to search the whole house. His favorite spot was in Huey's den, so she moved in that direction, praying that she was right.

Halfway there, she dropped to her hands and knees and crawled under the billowing smoke toward the heavy paneled door that led to the den. It felt cool, so she pushed inside. "Apache? Here, kitty, kit—" Her voice broke into a coughing spell, her lungs burning, her chest racked with pain. The air grew hotter, thinner, and she could barely get a deep breath. Frantically, she searched the smoke-filled room. *Where is he? Where is he?*

She was about to give up when she heard the soft mewling. She squinted through the smoke and saw two green eyes peering down from on top of the bookcase. Quickly, she pushed the desk chair against the shelves and clamored up, reaching for the cat.

It shrank away. She stretched onto her tiptoes. "Come on, come on."

In one final effort, she jumped and snatched it by the scruff, yanking it off the bookcase. The chair tipped, and she tumbled to the ground, the cat in her arms. It hissed and yelped and dug its claws into her flesh, but she hung on, determined not to let go. She darted back to the hallway, hesitated and decided the back door was closer than the front door at this point. Pulling Apache close, she ran through the smoke-filled kitchen and stumbled into the backyard, sucking in clean air.

"We made it, boy. It's okay," she said between breaths. "Huey's going to be so relieved to see—" She stopped.

A hooded figure was crouched among the shrubs with a gun pointed at her.

"This doesn't look good," Logan said, his mind reeling with horrific scenarios. He pleaded with God: *Please let everyone be okay. Let Emma be okay.*

Pruitt turned onto Huey's street and maneuvered through

the noisy swarm of emergency vehicles. First Huey's truck and now his home, Logan thought. He should have never asked for his friend's help. He'd brought evil raining down on him.

Pruitt screeched to a halt in front of the house, and Logan leaped out immediately. The sirens of the fire truck screamed closer with each second, but Logan and Pruitt had beaten them to the scene. He spotted Huey and several guys with a garden hose, spraying the side of the house. He sprinted toward them and was only halfway across the yard when Huey left the group and ran toward him. He waved his arms frantically. "Emma went back into the house after the cat."

He grabbed the older man by the shoulders. "When? How long ago?"

"Just a couple minutes ago. I told her not to, but she went anyway. She should be coming out any second." He pointed to the flames. "Fire's only in the garage, but the whole place is filled with smoke. We're hosing down the house now, hoping the fire doesn't take the rest of the place."

Logan looked at the home and the smoke pouring from the open front door. What was she thinking? Smoke was as deadly as fire. The sirens wailed even louder now as the fire truck approached, but would they be here in time? His mind filled with unwanted visions of Emma collapsed on the floor, gasping for air. He couldn't wait for the firefighters. Every second mattered.

He ran for the house, pulling off his shirt and tying it over his nose and mouth like a bandanna. He headed straight through the cloud of smoke and into the living room, feeling his way along the walls. "Emma!" Fumes seeped through the fabric and tasted scorched, his eyes stung, and tears streamed down his face. Coughing and gagging, he yelled again, "Emma!"

Thick smoke swallowed his surroundings, leaving him confused and disoriented. He stopped and spun toward the other direction, his hands extended outward. This was impossible. She could be anywhere in this house. *Lord, help me find her.*

Dropping to his hands and knees, he lowered his face and crawled along through the family room and into the kitchen, feeling for clues as he moved. "Emma!" he called again and again as sweat trickled down his forehead, mixing with smoke dust and clouding his vision. Nausea bubbled in his stomach as he struggled to suck in air. He needed to get out, but he couldn't leave... *Bam, bam, bam!*

Gunfire? The shock of other dangers merged with his fear of the fire. It was coming from the backyard.

He fumbled his way toward the sound, pushed open the back door and peered out. Lit by the flickering flames of the garage fire, he saw Emma crouched behind his truck. Fear overtook him, the sound of gunfire triggering unwanted memories. A familiar haze settled over his body, permeating his thoughts and transporting him back to his time in the army. To a different scene of death and destruction. He remained frozen in the past, exposed and vulnerable, until movement and a flash of dark clothing pulled him from his stupor. The shooter was closing in on Emma.

She cried out in terror.

Logan lunged forward, determined to protect her at all costs.

Bam, bam, bam...

Emma crouched behind the bumper, cringing at the horrid sound of gunfire. This was it. She was going to die. She pleaded with God, *Please no, please no, not yet. Not this way.* She heard a thump and then—

"Emma. It's me."

Startled, she recognized that voice. "Logan." She sprang up, darted forward and fell into his arms.

He hugged her tight, so tight, she wondered if he'd ever let her go.

"You're okay. You're okay," he whispered.

She looked beyond Logan and saw Pruitt standing several feet away with his pistol clutched in his hand. He glanced her way and then back to the alley, where the darkly clad figure was sprawled face-first over the asphalt. Another deputy came around the side of the house with his weapon drawn.

Logan released her, then turned his focus on Pruitt as he approached the perpetrator.

Pruitt reached the gunman and kicked aside the gun, stooping to check for a pulse. "Get the paramedics back here. He's bad." He pulled back the hood. Blond hair tumbled out, and he stumbled backward and screamed out, "I said get me the paramedics. Now! It's Davis!" He fell to his knees, turned her over and started pumping on her chest. "No, no, no! Don't you die. Don't die!"

Emma looked on in horror. This whole time Jess pretended to be her friend, but… Then Emma remembered their conversation at the coffee shop. Jess had said that she was the first on the scene at Daniel's murder.

Had Jess killed her brother? Nausea rolled in Emma's stomach.

She followed Logan's gaze back to where Pruitt huddled with the paramedics as they worked, one squeezing a handheld air bag placed over Jess's nose and mouth, the other applying pressure to her gunshot wound.

Several minutes passed, with first responders and law enforcement calling orders as they worked diligently to save Davis or fight the fire. Emma and Logan stood silently, the smoke and dying flickers of fire reflecting their muddled and saddened spirits. Finally, the team attending Davis stopped, and the two paramedics exchanged a look before double-checking her pulse and shaking their heads. Jess Davis was dead. Pruitt lowered his head and cried.

Emma looked away, unable to witness Pruitt's anguish. He'd shot one of his young deputies. She couldn't imagine the cruelty of it. Logan's arms encircled her shoulders, and she leaned into him. "Davis wanted to kill me. All this time, I thought she was a friend." She told him about the tracking device she'd found. She now knew for sure that Davis had placed it in the jacket. "She probably put other devices on our vehicles, and who knows where else."

"She must have tipped off Banks to our location at the mine," Logan said.

"It was probably Banks who shot at me out in the woods and burned up Daniel's Jeep, and tormented me in the cellar, but Davis was the insider in the sheriff's department. She had access to the ballistic reports, autopsies, original case file...everything. She was feeding information to Banks. Maybe she shot at us outside Crawford's place, too."

Apache wandered over. Emma scooped him up and held him close, taking comfort in his soft warmth.

"Why?" Logan asked. "How is Davis connected to all this?"

Emma shrugged. "I only know that she was out with Crawford and Mink the night Jack Murray was killed. Somehow Daniel must have connected her to his death. I barely had time to read through the files on the flash drive before the fire broke out. Maybe there's more..." She stroked the cat's chin and swallowed back her anger. "Davis acted so concerned about me. And so sad about Daniel's death. I bought into her act." Emma looked around. "She did this. She set fire to Huey's home to lure me out here so she could get me in the open and kill me. Just like she killed Daniel."

Logan drew her close. "You're safe," he said. "That's all that matters. You're safe."

Emma tipped her head until it rested against his shoulder, but her gaze remained on Pruitt as he knelt near Deputy Davis's body, his shoulders shaking with sobs.

She expected to feel an empathetic wave of Christian sympathy for this dead woman, caught in whatever mire of complex evils that propelled her to the lengths she'd taken. But part of her questioned: Was Deputy Davis's death a tragedy or justice well served?

She squeezed her eyes shut. The coldness of her own heart surprised her.

FIFTEEN

The sound of a ringtone pulled Emma from a deep sleep the next day. She reached for her phone and looked at the display. Afternoon? She'd slept until afternoon? And an unknown number? She shook herself awake, considered ignoring the call, but at the last second, she decided to answer.

"Ms. Hayes. This is Sheriff Pruitt."

She sat up. "Sheriff?"

"Wanted to let you know that we have Seth Murray in custody. He's not saying much. I've also been looking at the files from Daniel's investigation."

Emma threw off the comforter and stood, holding the phone to her ear as she paced back and forth in the tiny hotel room. Memories of yesterday cut through the fog in her brain: the fire, gunshots, Davis's death, being questioned by Pruitt and handing over the flash drive... It had been very late before she'd settled in for what was left of the night. After the fire, everyone from Huey's house had to find a new place to stay temporarily. Neighbors stepped up and offered their homes for the veterans, and Logan invited her to stay in Kate's room at the family home, but with Rachel's condition, she thought it was better to be on her own in a hotel. One of Huey's neighbors came to her rescue with a bag of used clothing and the use of her spare car.

Pruitt continued, "It looks like your brother uncovered a major drug trafficking route involving Murray Farms. I've reached out to federal agencies this morning and filled them in on his findings."

"Thank you. I'm surprised they're working on a Sunday afternoon." Emma felt a twinge of guilt at missing church.

"I called someone with the feds who I know personally, and it turns out that Daniel was on to something significant. They'd been trying to track down this distribution line for a long time."

Significant. Her heart kicked up a notch.

Pruitt continued, "We've been able to trace the connection between Banks and Seth Murray to about ten years ago."

"That's about the time Murray Mines went under."

"Right. Which makes sense. Murray would have been desperate for cash."

"But how—"

"I can't really go into much more detail right now, but I just felt I owed telling you this much."

"I've got a few questions for you." She went on to ask him about the horse auction photo and its relevance, and if he knew if any of this connected to the cold case murder of Jack Murray, or Jess Davis's relationship to Banks, and a half dozen other questions, most of which he wouldn't answer.

"You're persistent, Ms. Hayes. Probably what makes you a good reporter."

"Journalist. Investigative journalist."

"I'll give you this. That photo on Daniel's flash drive, the one that shows Seth at a horse auction?"

"Let me guess. Seth used the auctions as a cover for transporting drugs."

"We believe so. It's been done before. Horse trailers,

feed bins, vet supplies, these guys are clever. Or they think they are. Not sure how Daniel came about that photo, but it probably shows one of Seth's contacts. We're analyzing it and the rest of the flash drive contents now."

"Did Seth say anything about Kate?" she asked.

"We pressed him on that. He claims he doesn't know anything about what happened to her." He paused, and she heard kids' voices in the background. Grandkids? He continued, "I really can't say any more. I mostly called today to thank you. Daniel was up against some big players, and what he did was courageous. Drug trafficking is difficult to track, but if we bring down the system at the top, we can save a lot of lives. Your brother did good work."

Elation washed over Emma, belied by sadness. Daniel's work contributed to bringing down a multifaceted drug distribution network responsible for so much death and destruction. If only he was here to see the effects of his efforts. "Did Davis kill my brother?"

"I don't know for sure. We're still working on piecing everything together. But she was shooting a 9 mm bullet, the same that shot Crawford."

"And the same that Logan said he pulled from my brother's body."

"We're still looking into that. But it's possible. A couple of my deputies searched her place late last night, turned up some bank statements. She was receiving regular payments every month."

It was her. I know it was. Bitterness gripped Emma's heart. Daniel was betrayed by someone he thought was a friend. "What about the restaurant shooting? Did Jess own a gray sports car? Or Banks?"

"Nothing's turned up on the gray sports car yet. We'll come up with it soon. Be patient. And listen, all of this would make for good headlines, but keep it to yourself for now, okay? I don't want my investigation messed up. I'll let you know when you can run with the story. Are you going to be in the area for a while?"

Good question. It'd been over three weeks since Daniel had died. Her rent was due next week, plus utilities, internet, garbage, gym fees... "I'm going to have to head back to work soon," she said, surprised at how much she dreaded leaving. "Can't say when, for sure, but you can always reach me by phone."

"Sounds good. I'll be in touch and let you know what we figure out." They ended the call.

She sat back, and, for the first time in days, the despair that had hounded her from questions over Daniel's death and the anxiety of being stalked dissipated. Slowly they were replaced with relief at going back to some normalcy. Yet the thought of returning to her previous comfort zone in DC meant leaving River Falls, and a pang of something—regret, sadness, loss—quickly followed. If she were honest with herself, it was the realization that she would be leaving Logan. His life was here, and she'd come to understand and accept that, but something in her had shifted. Only she didn't know what to do about it. She pushed those thoughts aside, choosing for now to rest in knowing that she was safe, and that many of the questions shrouding Daniel's death had been answered.

She tugged off the baggy sweatshirt and sweatpants she'd found in a bag of clothing that was given to her by one of Huey's neighbors. Her own clothes were saturated with soot and smoke. She fished a pair of jeans and a sweater out of the bag, showered and finished dressing as Logan arrived with coffee and food.

"Hope you don't mind," he said, setting everything down

on the desk. "I know it's after lunch, but I haven't had break-fast yet."

She grabbed a bacon-and-egg sandwich, took a bite and spoke with her mouth full. "Thanks. I'm starved."

"Went by and saw my sister this morning after early services."

"How is she?"

"The bleeding stopped, but the doctor wants her to take it easy for a while. He sent her home on bed rest."

"I'll call her a little later. Is there anything she needs?"

"Prayers."

Emma glanced away and nodded.

"They did a scan at the hospital, and I can hardly believe it, but she's having twins."

"Twins?" Emma's heart soared, then fell. Twins, like she and—

"Stopped by Huey's, too," he said.

She swallowed and reached for one of the coffees. "You did? When did you sleep?"

"Didn't really. Anyway, the garage is a complete loss, but it could have been worse. Huey's looking for a temporary place for everyone to stay together until the smoke damage is cleaned up. Probably be a few weeks before they can move back in."

Emma grimaced. "I'm so sorry about all of this. I never would have wished any of this for Huey and the others."

"I am, too. I can't imagine Davis's motivation for everything she's done."

"Maybe we'll know more soon," Emma said. "Pruitt called me first thing this morning. They've arrested Seth. He was heading for the southern border."

His eyes went round. "Did Pruitt get him to say anything about Kate?"

"No. I'm sorry." Sadness clouded his features, and Emma quickly went on to tell him about the feds being called and Murray Farms being linked to drug trafficking, and the matching gun calibers. "Pruitt did confirm that Davis was shooting a 9 mm handgun, the same caliber that you said killed Daniel. She was also receiving monthly deposits from an unknown source. Although he doesn't have enough to connect Davis directly to Daniel's death yet."

"He will. It'll just take time."

Emma nodded. "I think she was on Seth's payroll. He paid her to kill my brother. And probably to keep silent all these years about Mink's alibi."

"Looks that way."

"Is Crawford doing any better? If he's off the ventilator, he might be able to talk."

"I'll call and find out this morning. I'll call Lillian, too. I can't believe Seth would get involved in something like drug trafficking. This will devastate her. That worries me, with her health the way it is."

"Me, too. And we're still missing the pieces that tie Davis and Banks to Jack Murray's homicide."

Logan agreed. "Yeah, we know the *who*, just not the *why* and *how*. And I can't help but think that once we have those answers, we'll know what happened to Kate." He stood and stretched. "So what do we do next?"

"What do you mean?"

"About these unanswered questions. What's our strategy?"

Strategy? Emma's heart fell. How was she going to tell Logan that she had to go home? "I don't have a strategy. I need to go see my parents for a couple days and then head back to DC."

He looked like he'd just been punched in the gut.

"I can't stay away from work forever. I've got bills to pay and…"

His features turned cold. He crumpled his sandwich wrapper and shot it into the nearby wastebasket.

"It's just that now we know that we can trust Pruitt and he has the file with the information, and feds are involved, we'll find out the rest eventually."

"Yeah, eventually."

She reached out. "Logan, I—"

He stepped back and held up his hand. "Don't. It's okay. Really." He turned his back, gathered up the rest of their breakfast garbage and tossed it in the wastebasket.

"Are you leaving? I still have a couple days here, and I thought maybe we could do something together."

"Not today. I'd better spend some time with my family and catch up on my own work." His last two words rang with an edge of *I have a life, too, you know*, and she started to feel defensive when he turned and met her gaze. His dark eyes glistened, and his lips quivered ever so slightly now with unspoken words. The gaze of the man who had saved her life, who had made her feel life again, now stared at her face for a couple of extra beats, as if he was drinking in everything about her. He started to say something, and Emma waited, every part of her anticipating his words. Would he ask her to stay? She'd thought about it over and over the past few days, what he meant to her and what she would give up for him. But he hesitated, darkness crossing over his features, and then he turned and walked toward the door without so much as a goodbye.

Emma watched him go. Should she follow? Would he change his mind and come back? Seconds slipped into minutes without either happening. She stood alone in the silence of the room, staring at the closed door and wondering if she'd just made the biggest mistake of her life.

Logan stomped on the gas pedal, gravel shooting out from under his tires. Quickly, he slowed, shaking his head at acting like a stupid teenager.

Part of him wanted to take back or at least regret everything that he'd felt and had said. But, no, he sighed. He didn't regret how he felt for Emma. She had brought so much into his life: a sense of purpose in uncovering the truth, a need to resolve his own issues of faith, and most of all, love. After all these years, he'd allowed himself to trust a woman again. A woman who was like none other. And maybe that was the problem. A noted and respected journalist like Emma had a life to lead beyond these mountains and this small town. It was evident that she loved her life in the city, her friends, her career. She had proved herself as capable, resilient and, yes, just the kind of woman he wanted in his life. But there was more she needed to do, more stories to write and a world of journalism still ahead of her.

What she left behind was a legacy that he would always treasure. She had stood as a testament to perseverance and a willingness to pursue the truth at any cost. And the truth was that he was now a better man than the one who had spied that swatch of color on the shore of Blackwater River.

As the miles rolled by, he knew he had a lot of work to do. A free clinic that required, as always, resources to help those afflicted with illness and addictions. He could always hope that the scope of the drug scourge would be abated by the arrest of those like Seth, but he was realistic, as well. Realistic enough to know that his clinic would always need him. And that running from the truth would never save him from the guilt over Daniel's death. Only faith could help him through that. And he was also realistic enough to know that with more clarity now, a gift from Emma, he could lead a better life.

Even though it would be without her.

SIXTEEN

Emma slid the grocery bag onto the counter and admonished her friend, "Don't you dare get off that sofa. You're supposed to be on bed rest."

Rachel leaned back into the cushion and shook her head, rubbing her hand over her growing belly. "This is making me so antsy. I'm not good at resting."

Emma laughed. "Enjoy it while you can. You won't get any rest after the babies are born." She unpacked the grocery bag. "Look at what I brought. Not one, but two pints of ice cream. Chocolate chip cookie dough for you, strawberry for me." She pulled two spoons from the drawer and joined Rachel on the couch. "Thought we could eat straight from the containers."

"Why not?" Rachel took the ice cream and rolled her eyes. "I'm going to be huge."

"That's a given. Twins. I can't believe it. They'll be best of friends, just like Daniel and..." Emma's voice trailed off.

"Oh, Emma. I know you miss him. I'm so sorry."

It hurt to think of her brother. Hopefully there would come a time when she could remember good memories fondly and without so much pain. "Thank you. I wish you could have met him. He was the best brother ever." She blinked back the tears forming. "But this is my last day here, and I want to celebrate with you, not talk about sad things. I am incredibly happy for you and Joe. And the babies." She held up her ice cream container for a toast. "Here's to a lifetime of happiness, times two. No doubt that you'll be the most amazing parents ever."

They savored the first few bites of their ice cream in silence. Then Rachel brought up the elephant in the room. "Have you talked to Logan since yesterday?"

"No." She'd been hopeful for a call or at least a text, but nothing. "He was so angry when he left."

"He isn't mad at you, just the situation. You know, him here, you in DC. I think he was wishing that you'd stick around."

Emma didn't know what to say. Something had changed inside her during her time spent in this small mountain town. She loved the open sky, the dense forests, the friendly waves from strangers. She'd miss it here. More than that, she'd miss Logan. A lot.

"He's in love with you," Rachel said. "Madly in love."

Emma quickly took another bite of ice cream. And then another.

"Did you hear me?" Rachel asked. "My brother's in love with you, and it's obvious that you love him, too. Don't ya?"

Emma nodded. "Yes. Very much so."

"Then the only thing holding you two back is that you're both stubborn and set in your ways. What a shame that one of you can't compromise." Rachel grabbed a tissue and dabbed at a dribble of ice cream on the fabric covering her protruding stomach. "Honestly, I'm worried about Logan."

"You are?"

"He's lovesick for you, but he's struggling with a lot of financial pressure with the clinic. The Murray Farms fund-raiser is off, obviously, and that was always a huge moneymaker for him. Without Lillian's support, I don't know if the clinic will be able to keep its doors open. And he was counting on there being a development about Kate's disappearance. He built himself up for it and now he's taking it hard. I get it. We're no closer to understanding what happened to her. And we were both so hopeful."

Emma reached over and touched Rachel's hand. "I know you must be so disappointed. I'm sorry, but don't give up. With the flash drive evidence, they have enough to go after Seth. He'll eventually talk. Then you'll get your answers."

"I'm not so sure. I never realized how greedy he really was, to resort to drug trafficking. Just think of all the harm he's done to other people. I know it's not been proven yet, but if he did kill Jack…poor Lillian. I couldn't think of anything worse than burying a child, and to know that your other child was responsible for the death and is now going to prison. It'd be too much to endure."

Too much to endure. Emma stared at where Rachel's hands rested on her belly and thought of the two children side by side, encapsulated in the safety and warmth of their mother's womb. All a mother ever wanted was to protect her children. It was instinctual, primal. Even animals had the same… The mare and the foal… She frowned. Could it be?

Emma stood and wrapped her arms around Rachel. "I've got to go. I'll call you later, okay?"

"So fast? Did I say something?"

"No. That's not it at all. Just rest. I'll explain later. I promise."

Emma hurried out the door, her mind putting together the pieces as she went. She called Pruitt on the way to the clinic. He was going to contact a judge and get a bench warrant issued and meet her at Murray Farms in two hours with a human remains detection dog and handler.

The compact on loan from Huey's neighbor was great for quick errands but chugged on the steep West Virginia hills. By the time she got to the clinic, she was a frustrated mess at the interminably slow trek. She rushed inside to find several mothers with crying babies and red-cheeked toddlers filling the chairs that lined the waiting room wall, along with a middle-aged woman scrolling on her phone and an older gentleman stooped over his walker. No one was at the reception desk, so Emma spun in a circle, unsure of what to do.

"Take a seat," a harried mother told her. "Doc Greer is on his own today. He's calling us back in order. I'm next." She jostled her screaming infant with one hand and wiped her toddler's snotty nose with the other. Emma took a seat across the room.

Ten minutes later, Logan appeared with a chart in his hand. "Mrs.— Emma?"

Emma crossed the room. "I need to talk to you."

He pointed to his patients. "I'm a little busy."

"It's important. Really important. Please. It's about Kate."

The harried mother came over with both kids, the infant's cries piercing. "I've been waiting longer than her. And I've got sick kids."

Logan nodded to the mother. "I'm sorry, Mrs. Brian. The first room on the right. I'll be right in."

The mother gave Emma a disapproving up and down as she clutched her infant and wrangled her toddler down the hall to the examination room. Even from behind closed doors, the baby's screams still rang throughout the clinic.

"I'll be quick," Emma said. "Pruitt is sure about the connection between Seth and Banks and the drug trafficking, but Seth denies any involvement with Kate's disappearance."

"Don't tell me you believe Seth Murray. He's a—"

"I think he may be telling the truth about Kate. He doesn't know what happened to her because he didn't have anything to do with her disappearance. But Lillian may have—"

"Lillian? No. You're mistaken. That can't be true."

Emma touched Logan's arm. "Just hear me out. We both believe that Seth killed Jack over the drug deals. Right?"

He nodded.

"Well, what if Kate saw it happen? And Lillian killed Kate to protect Seth? Think about it. Lillian was there that night. If Kate witnessed the killing, she would have been terrified. She might have run to Lillian. She trusted her. You told me that she and your mother were friends."

Logan shook his head. "But Lillian would never do such a thing. She's been so good to me all these years. One of the few people who believed in me after Kate was accused of… No. No. She would never do something like that to me."

"Davis was being paid to keep quiet. We just assumed it was Seth who was paying her off. It could have been Lillian paying for her silence all these years. Davis was probably easily bought. Kate wouldn't have been. Lillian knew that. In her mind, she didn't have a choice. Kate or her only surviving son."

Logan's face flushed red. "No. You're wrong about this."

"A foal was being buried that day…"

"No. No."

"Pruitt's getting a warrant issued to search the farm. He's going to meet us in two hours with a dog handler." Another infant scream burst through the closed door on the right. Emma moved closer and took Logan by the shoulders. "I hope I'm wrong about all this. Maybe I am, but we need to find out once and for all. Let me help you finish up here and then we can go out to Murray Farms. Together."

* * *

It was late afternoon when they reached the farm. Pruitt arrived before them with a team of people and a warrant. They had brought in digging equipment and were waiting on the dog and handler to arrive.

Rachel had sent Joe, and the three of them stood together under an oak tree in the corner of the pasture. The perfect blue of the sky and the dried orange oak leaves still clinging to wide branches contrasted with the white fence, painting an almost perfect picture. Emma thought it was as if God was consoling them by providing so much beauty in such an ugly moment.

"This is ridiculous," Lillian was saying. She had aged in a matter of days, her eyes dull and her mouth downturned on sagging jowls. "You're not going to find anything out here except the remains of a dead horse." She shook her fist at Logan. "How can you do this to me? After all I've done for you. And now, even as my son has been arrested. My only living son." Lillian's voice sounded shrill against the crisp air. "Don't do this to me, Logan. Make this stop."

Logan stared straight ahead, ignoring Lillian, his jaw twitching. Emma placed her arm around him, trying to provide what comfort she could. Joe was speaking softly over the phone, doing the same for Rachel.

They all turned at the sound of another car pulling up. "It's the canine handler," Pruitt said.

"You people are making a huge mistake," Lillian burst out. "How dare you make these accusations. Who do you people think you are? Without me and my family, none of you would even have jobs. And don't you think for one second, Dr. Greer, that you'll ever get another penny for that clinic of yours. Never!"

No one was listening to her. Instead, their gazes were

trained on the young woman who approached with a shep-
herd on a leash. She introduced herself as Ivy and her dog,
Rio. Rio's soulful eyes and mild manners captivated Emma.

Pruitt had already mapped out a grid over the search
area for the handler. She spent a few minutes walking Rio
along the outer perimeter of the area, then gave him more
lead as she methodically led him over each part of the grid.
Rio worked back and forth, his nose down, frantically sniff-
ing every inch of the ground. It didn't take long before he
stopped and sat, rigid and unmoving, his gaze intense. An
alert, Emma knew. He'd detected human remains.

She felt Logan's body tremble. She glanced at his profile and saw tears running down his face. He turned and
looked at Lillian. Before Emma could stop him, he charged
forward. "Is it her?" he shouted. "Is it her?"

Lillian stared at him, arms folded, face twisted in anger.
Joe stepped aside, his phone to his ear, his voice low and
broken as he talked to Rachel, her muffled sobs audible
over the line.

"We'll know soon enough," Pruitt said. "We're going to
dig up every inch of dirt in this area."

"Is it her?" Logan asked, his voice less angry and more
pleading.

Lillian raised both her fists and shook them at the sky.
"I had no choice. Don't you understand? No choice!"

Her words hung in the still air.

"Yes, you did," Logan choked out. "We all have a choice."

SEVENTEEN

It was dark by the time Logan pulled in next to Emma in the hotel parking lot. He'd stayed until his sister's remains were excavated, Emma by his side, never wavering. For years he'd prepared himself for the moment he'd know the truth about Kate, and now that it was here, he was gutted, his emotions raw.

"Are you doing okay?" Emma asked, as he opened her car door.

"I'm numb."

She grasped his hand and held it firm as they walked toward her room in the middle of an L-shaped lineup of rickety doors. The Blue Mountain Motel was the oldest—and now only—lodging in town, and ever since the Murrays built the Grand Lodge on the mountain, it'd fallen into disrepair.

"There's no need for you to be alone out here," he said. "You should have stayed with Joe and Rachel."

"They've got enough going on without a houseguest adding to the mix."

She was right. He imagined Joe and Rachel tucked away in their home, holding each other, comforting one another. The truth around Kate's death held spikes of pain that would take years to blunt. Knowing his sister's fate may start a healing process, but the actual healing could take a lifetime. At least Joe and Rachel had each other and the solace of each other's arms, as well as the bright light of a future with a growing family. He, however, had never felt more alone in his life. "Are you still leaving tomorrow?"

"I thought I'd stay a couple more days before going to see my parents. They need me to be home for a little while, but I also want to be here for you and Rachel."

"And after that?"

They stopped at her door. She looked up, the flashing light from a motel sign casting strange shadows over her face. "I don't know. I love my work and I need to pay my bills, but talking to Rachel today and thinking about Daniel's death has made me realize that I need to rethink my priorities. I've been too caught up in my work."

"Is that a bad thing? You have an amazing career."

"I don't know. Somewhere along the way, I've lost my perspective on what I've been doing and why. I've watched you at the clinic, how you care for folks, and you don't do it for a byline or special recognition."

"Bringing down someone like Victor Duran has saved—"

"I know, and it sounds noble, what I've achieved with my journalism, but in all honesty, that's not what's been driving me. I've been forced to face the truth about myself as we've struggled with life and death over these last days. And I know now I've been chasing fame and recognition, blindly sacrificing other aspects of my life to achieve it. I've surrendered time with my brother, my parents, and I regret every moment that I failed to share with them."

Logan nodded. "I understand about seeing things more clearly now. I realize I've submerged my grief and pain in a hectic life, what with my job, the clinic. But for me, helping others is more than just a cover-up for my personal issues. It has been my small way to give solace to others. I've been so blessed."

She grew quiet.

"Did I say something wrong?"

"No. It's just...how can you still feel blessed? After all this with Kate? And the way Lillian betrayed you. Don't you ever feel angry? Angry at the world, angry at God?"

Logan swallowed hard. "Yes, I have. And I still do from time to time. It creeps up when I least expect it. But I try to focus on the good, to do good, or the best that I can. And yes, to see the blessings, even the fleeting ones." He looked at her, his eyes searching hers. "In the midst of it all, I've had these few days with you."

She burst into tears. He pulled her close and felt her body tremble against his. He brushed his lips over her hair and closed his eyes, certain that her tears streamed from her loss of Daniel, a tragedy that he knew he was partly to blame for.

He put distance between them, yet looked into her eyes, every ounce of him wanting to kiss away her tears, but he held back. "There's something I need to tell you. It's about Daniel. I should have told you this earlier. I just didn't know how."

She was working hard to find peace with her brother's death. What he was about to say might destroy that peace as well as ruin his chances with her. She was the last person he ever wanted to cause any pain. But he had to tell her everything. For his sake as well as for hers.

"I struggle with war memories. Certain things trigger flashbacks for me, and it's like I travel outside my body. Everything slows. I'm not myself. It is like being in a catatonic dream state. I've had enough therapy to understand it is the mind's way of distancing the person from unbearable pain. But understanding it doesn't stop it."

She nodded, kindly, gently, urging him to go on. "I've seen that happen to you. I saw it the day Crawford was shot."

He nodded, recalling. "Gunfire is a trigger."

"But you didn't hesitate to protect me when Davis was shooting at me."

"No, I didn't have a flashback then, but I did the night Daniel came into the ER. His gunshot wound took me back to my medic days. Times in the field with gunfire all around and us medics rushing in and…" He looked at her with eyes that pleaded for mercy. "There were things that I saw back then, things that no one should ever witness."

She touched his cheek. "You don't have to tell me this. It's okay."

"No. I do. I want you to know the truth. When I was operating on Daniel, I had a flashback and the paralysis hit me, everything slowed, and my hand, I couldn't even move my hand." He lifted his right hand, and she gently took it in her fingers. "I hesitated. If I… If he'd had another doctor, he might have stood a better chance."

She held still for a moment, her fingers still gentle on his hand. Was she envisioning him standing in the surgery room, paralyzed as Daniel died? Would she lash out at him, blame him just as he blamed himself?

"I don't believe that." Her words came out firm but soft. "I know you did everything you could. It just wasn't meant to be."

"Didn't you hear me? I hesitated and it may have cost your brother his life."

"I've struggled a lot with Daniel's death, and with my faith, and still do. Every day. But Daniel worked so hard to shed light in the darkness and bring justice into others' lives, and he must have completed all that God had planned for him."

Logan shook his head. "But I didn't save him because of my—"

"No." She moved her hands to touch them tenderly to his face. "I believe that you did everything you could to save my brother. Jess Davis is responsible for his death. Not you. I told you before that I wouldn't have wanted any other doctor with Daniel in his final moments. I meant it then. And I still do."

He met her gaze briefly and then looked away. Her abrupt green eyes held sincerity and love, not anger and judgment.

"Let it go, Logan."

She had already forgiven him. Could he forgive himself?

He took a step back and turned away. "I should be going. Good night, Emma."

The raw pain of Logan's confession left Emma bone tired. She stumbled into her motel room and stood, staring at herself in the mirror over the dresser. She raised her hand to her face. Pale, eyes sunken, ugly bruises under yellow caked makeup. A slash down one cheek and even Apache's claw marks across her arm. She glanced at her nails and then to the polish and file on the dresser and said to the mirror, "Why bother? There's no fixing this mess."

Not just beaten but deflated. Part of her wanted to slip under the covers and forget everything, but even though her body was exhausted, her mind still spun on overdrive, whirling with theories about Seth's motivations, the drug-dealing operation and its murderous consequences.

She sighed and flipped on the television, where a young news anchor spoke about a body found at Murray Farms. So far, they had little to report, not even Kate's name and not any information on Seth or Jess Davis. *But it won't be long before the whole story breaks.* Emma felt a familiar itch to get a jump on other reporters, even though she'd promised Pruitt she wouldn't release certain facts yet. It was the part of her that had propelled her for years, the same part that had kept her from the more important things in life. Fame over relationships, reputation over time with loved ones. Did she really want to spend the next several years on the fast track, sacrificing her life and what little time she might have with her parents? And…sacrificing her chance at a relationship with Logan? Was she really done with the world of competitive journalism? Or was she kidding herself that she could ever "settle down" to a normal life?

She tried to convince herself of the reality that what they'd turned up over these tumultuous days had revealed something that satisfied the personal void that she—and Logan—had needed filled. Maybe she never would have all the answers about Daniel's and Kate's murders, but at least her parents would know the identity of the person responsible for their son's death, and that Jess Davis was no longer able to hurt anyone else. And Lillian would be arrested and tried for her part in Kate's death. On top of that, another drug supply chain was disrupted and dismantled. All good things. Emma should feel peace, yet she felt more restless than ever.

She turned off the television and decided that a hot shower would calm her nerves and warm her up. It was freezing in this room. She turned the thermostat up a couple of notches and pulled a pair of crumpled sweats from the bag of used clothing, then opened her music app as she crossed the room to the bathroom, scrolling her playlist for some soft music—

"You're a hard woman to kill." A man had emerged from her bathroom pointing a gun at her. Behind him, the bathroom window hung ajar, forced open.

A scream formed in her mouth but came out as a small shriek, tight and squeaky, bone-dry. Before she could move, he charged forward and pushed the gun against her forehead. Her vision filled with his ugly face: splotchy pitted skin, a gold tooth under dry lips, a tattooed snake creeping around his neck. His eyes two black pits, lacking emotion, as if killing her meant nothing to him. "Victor sent me. He wants you to pay for what you did to him."

The cold steel of the barrel slid across her skin, sending fear coursing through her veins. Tangy sweat filled the air, stung her nostrils. She gagged and shifted her gaze away from his face, her eyes catching briefly on her sharp nail file perched on the edge of the dresser. *Grab the file. Do it!* But she couldn't. It was too far away, and he'd shoot her before she could get her hands on it.

He let out an impatient sigh. "Let's get this done. Turn around and kneel."

"Please, God, no."

His lips curled into a half-crazed smile. "Ain't nobody gonna help you now. Especially not God."

Logan returned to his car and cranked the engine. His cell rang. "Hey, Sheriff. What's going on?"

"I know it's late," Pruitt said on the other end. "We've had a couple of developments. Banks is dead. But before he passed, he recovered enough to give a statement about Lillian paying him to frame Mink. We used it to get a full confession from Lillian."

Logan gripped the steering wheel with his other hand and leaned forward.

Pruitt cleared his throat. "Turns out she knew all along that Seth was bringing in money illegally and suspected it had to do with drugs. She said they were in desperate financial straits after the mine closed."

"As if that justifies anything."

"I'm just telling you what she said. Anyway, she said that Kate was at the barn that night, trying to calm down a mare who'd just lost her foal, when an argument broke out between Jack and Seth. Jack had apparently discovered his brother's side business and was furious."

"If you remember Jack, he pretty much played by the rules."

"Yeah," Pruitt agreed. "Guess so. He threatened to call the cops, and Seth blew up, lost control and picked up a gun and shot him. Kate saw the whole thing go down and was terrified."

Logan stared through the windshield at the night sky. "She went to Lillian for help, and Lillian killed her."

"I'm sorry, Logan." Pruitt's voice cracked over the line. "She claims she was in shock over hearing that Jack was dead, was afraid for Seth, on and on, but the truth is she killed Kate to protect Seth."

"All these years," Logan bit out, "I've thought of Lillian as a friend." It was all he could do to control the anger that threatened to suck him into a dark abyss. "How'd she do it?"

Pruitt hesitated.

"Tell me. I want to know all of it."

"She stabbed her, wrapped her body in a blanket and dragged her outside. It was dark, Seth had already run from the farm, and there was no one else around, so she used the backhoe to dump Kate's body into the foal's grave and cover it with dirt. She removed Kate's necklace and planted it at the scene."

"Then she paid Banks to frame Mink?"

"Yep. And bought off Crawford and Davis, too. Later, Davis became an asset to her in the police department."

Logan clenched his phone. "She let an innocent man go to prison for killing my sister." He paused, then asked, "Did she admit to hiring Davis to kill Daniel?"

"Uh-huh, she did. And Crawford, too." Logan heard Pruitt take a breath before he added, "We're still working to exonerate Mink for Kate's death. With everything we have, it shouldn't take long."

Every ounce of energy drained from Logan's body. *And the truth shall set you free.* But for now, the truth only deepened the sorrow over Kate's death and the twisted path of crimes that followed it.

Logan turned the phone to speaker and set it on the passenger seat, as if too tired to even hold it, yet he wanted— needed—all the facts. "What about Salieri, the attorney? He must have been in on it," he asked as he backed out of his parking space.

"He's moved on to Charlotte and is in private practice. We're checking into him, but it's going to be hard to prove he did anything wrong in his defense of Mink."

"So much evil," Logan said. Brother turning against brother over greed and selfishness, ruining the lives of so many. He exited the lot and turned the corner, his headlights catching on a car parked in the alley behind the motel. He stopped and shoved the gear into Reverse, backing up until his lights hit the vehicle again. His knuckles went white on the steering wheel—it was the gray sports car.

Emma moved slowly, her legs heavy, her heart full of fear. *Please, God, please.* She asked God to help her parents and Logan and everyone she loved.

The man snarled, "Hurry up. I don't have all night."

Will it hurt? Will Daniel be waiting? She bent one knee, regrets skittering through her mind, a future lost and a past wasted. Had she done enough with her life? And her parents, her poor parents! And Logan. He would never know that she loved him.

"Please don't do this," she pleaded, squeezing her eyes shut as she pressed both knees into the shag carpet.

A sound came from deeper in the unit—the bathroom.

Emma's eyes popped open, and she turned just in time to see the man jerk around and point the gun at the bathroom. "Who's in there?"

Her view slid from his back to the nail file, and her heart rate kicked into high speed.

She bolted from the floor, seized the fingernail file and plunged it into the side of his neck. His scream set fire to every nerve in her body as the gun fell from his hand. She dived for it, only to catch a backhand to the side of her face. The blow sent her stumbling into the dresser. She slid to the floor and looked upward to see the file protruding above the man's collar at an odd angle. His face twisted in pain and hate and evil determination as he snatched up the gun and jammed it into her face. "It's going to be such a pleasure to kill you."

Adrenaline coursed through every vein in Logan's body as he sprang, with two quick steps into the room, and faced a horrific scene—Emma on the ground slumped against the dresser with a gun pressed against her head.

"No!" Logan shouted and threw all his weight into the man's back. They hit the floor with a thud, a tangle of arms and legs, grunting and panting, as they fought for control of the gun. Logan gained control, the man gained an edge, and then the gun suddenly fired.

Logan froze, paralyzed as he witnessed the life drain from the other man's eyes, his own mind replaying wartime memories: a young soldier caught in an IED explosion, flailing, his side a mangle of flesh, his body bleeding out…

"Logan?" Emma's voice sounded as if from the depth of a well, distant and haunting.

He stilled, blinked several times, and his mind focused on the blood soaking the carpet around him. The sight of so much blood threatened to take him down the black hole again.

"Logan!" Her arms enveloped him and gently led him outside and away from the scene. "Logan, it's okay. You're here with me. You saved me." She pressed her face into his shoulder, as if trying to erase the horror of it all. Would that even be possible? he wondered. Would either of them be able to get past the trauma of these past days?

"How did you know to come back?" she asked.

"I was talking to Pruitt when I saw the gray sports car parked behind the motel. I pulled in to check it out. The window was forced open."

"It was one of Victor Duran's men. He's the one who shot at us in the restaurant."

Sirens wailed in the distance. "Pruitt told me to wait until deputies arrived, but—"

"If you'd waited, he would have killed me." She lifted her face to his. "When the gun was pressed against my head, my only thoughts were of you. Of us. Together. I thought I was going to die in that hotel room, and all I could think of…was that I might not see—"

"Shh." He took her other hand in his and clasped their palms together as if in a prayer held true and tight between them. "I understand. You were the only thing that filled my mind. The only one who can ever fill my heart.

I...I love you, Emma, and I want to be with you, no matter what it takes."

She looked deep into his eyes, "And I love you, Logan. And I'm willing to go anywhere, live anywhere, to be with you."

He released her hands, and with her words echoing in his mind, he tenderly drew her forward until their lips met.

The sirens grew louder, and clouds parted, revealing the bright night sky.

EPILOGUE

Six months later, Emma sat with Logan on his front porch, looking at another night sky. Rachel was nearing full term and the doctor had allowed her to go back to her normal activities. She'd insisted on serving them a home-cooked meal and then shooed them outside, saying she'd call them in when dessert was ready. Emma knew it was to give her and Logan a bit of time alone.

The months since the attack in her hotel room had been busy for Emma. After a quick visit with her parents, she'd returned to DC to wrap up a couple of work projects and sublet her apartment. Back in River Falls, she'd rented a room while she did some freelance writing and slowly renovated Daniel's cabin. Maybe one day she would live there. Especially now that Victor Duran was no longer a threat to her. He'd been found dead in his cell, a victim of yet another drug lord's vindictiveness.

Seth's arrest and Victor Duran's death had sparked the interest of an editor from a national news source. He'd reached out and asked Emma for a spin-off of her original Victor Duran article, including several pieces on local corruption and drug trafficking. But after experiencing so much crime and violence firsthand, she'd found the assignment too difficult to write. Instead, she'd put together a human-interest piece on compassion and service, which featured Huey's home for veterans. She didn't know if the editor would accept it, but she thought it was some of her best work yet.

Logan reached for her hand. "I received a letter today," he began. "Kind of a surprise, to say the least."

Emma cocked her head. "A good surprise or...?"

"It seems," he continued, a smile growing on his lips, "that someone wrote a grant to the state for an assistance program. It's for medical practices, like mine, that offer care for low-income populations."

"I can't believe it went through! I should have told you, but it seemed like a long shot. I wrote it after everything that happened. After Lillian pulled her financial support. I just wanted to help. I know your life is devoted to this town, these people, and your clinic does so much good."

"Help? You've saved the clinic. It's enough money to keep us in the black for at least two years. Thank you, Emma."

"Rachel helped, too. She got me all the information I needed." Emma hesitated and drew in a deep breath. "Speaking of Lillian," she said. "Not to be a downer, but her trial starts next week."

He nodded. "I know. I've been praying for her."

"Me, too. I just wish I knew why she—"

"I don't think we'll ever know. There are things that we can't understand in this lifetime. I'm just grateful for the answers we did uncover."

Logan was right. She needed to let it go and simply be grateful. She sighed and lifted her gaze to the night sky. A slight breeze rustled the blossoms of a nearby lilac bush, releasing a sweet scent into the spring air, reminding Emma of the lilacs outside her mother's kitchen window—memories from a love-filled childhood. Family could be the saving grace for some people, or their ultimate downfall. She really did have much to be grateful for—so many blessings. And even though she missed Daniel, she trusted that she would see him again—

Logan cleared his throat, and she realized her mind had drifted. She looked at him and saw him chewing his lip, trying to form a statement. Or maybe a question.

Her heart rate quickened. Just this morning her prayers had taken her to Isaiah and the verse *When the time is right, I, the Lord, will make it happen.*

Could it be? All these months, she'd been waiting and hoping and praying.

He released her hand and stood, removing a ring from his jean pocket. Her heart swelled as he knelt before her.

"Emma. I thank God every day for putting you in my life. And I want to be with you, no matter where that is, for all my life. I love you, Emma. Will you be my wife?"

"Oh, Logan. Yes." A tear ran down Emma's cheek as she slid forward in her chair and flung her arms around his neck.

At that very moment, the screen door swung open, and Joe burst through, saying, "It's time!"

Logan looked at his brother-in-law with a grin on his face. "We'll be in for dessert soon."

"No! Time! The twins are coming!"

"What? They aren't due until—"

But Joe had already disappeared back inside the house. Logan looked at the ring still in his palm and laughed. "That wasn't the best timing."

Emma stood and pulled Logan up beside her, taking the ring from his hand and slipping it onto her finger. "I'd say the time is right," she said. "For everything."

* * * * *

Dear Reader,

No one escapes grief. At some point in our lives, we all encounter loss. Loss of a parent, a spouse, a child, marriage or our own health. Grief is painful. I think it's supposed to be, because sometimes we must feel pain to grow through it, especially in our faith.

Our sufferings remind us of how Christ suffered out of love for us. If we unite our own pain to His sufferings on the cross, it brings us closer to Him. But it's easy to believe the opposite—that if we are suffering, God must be against us. And instead of growing closer to Him, we distance ourselves like Emma, in my story, who experiences a spiritual crisis after the death of her twin brother. We see her wrestle with her faith and become embittered. She blames God and wants nothing to do with Him. But God never lets go of her, and throughout the story, we get to watch her grow, overcome her anger and learn to trust Him again.

I've experienced firsthand how life's tragedies can knock us off our faith track. That's why I chose Deuteronomy 31:8 as the Scripture verse to open this story—*It is the Lord who goes before you; he will be with you and will never fail you or forsake you. So do not fear or be dismayed.* These words remind me that God is a faithful, loving father who never forgets His children. This gives me great courage and comfort. I hope it does the same for you.

Thank you for reading Emma and Logan's story. I'm grateful for the opportunity to share it with you.

Reach out to me anytime through social media or via my website's contact page at www.susanfurlong.com. I'd love to hear from you!

Susan